SETTLING IN NAZARETH

BY SANDY DELUCA

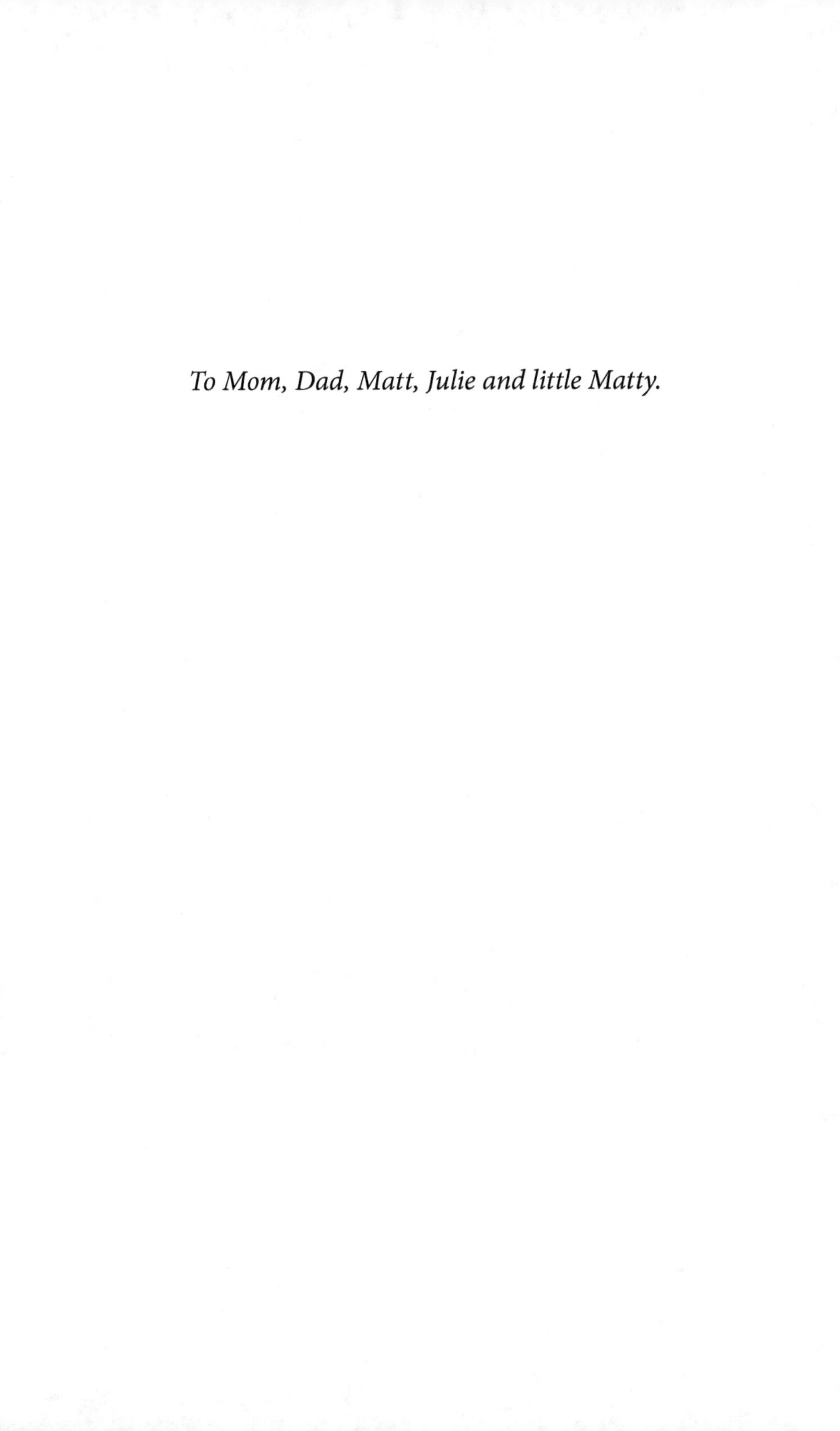

To Mom, Dad, Matt, Julie and little Matty.

AUTHOR NOTES

This book was conceived in 2001, most of it written after September 11th. Since that time, technology has advanced and items mentioned, such as VCRs, are no longer in vogue. It had a very limited paperback print run, often finding its way into Delirium Books promotional giveaways—and only listed for sale with several small retailers. I am thankful that Crossroad Press published this book in digital format in 2017, and in paperback in 2018.

Please note that my character Detective Mansi made an appearance in my novella MESSAGES FROM THE DEAD. Over the years I've thought about doing a follow-up book starring my protagonist Ruby. Maybe that will come to be in the future. Nazareth is a fictional city. If it were a reality, it would exist in Southern Rhode Island, somewhere by Narragansett.

Thanks to David Niall Wilson, David Dodd, and the editorial staff at Crossroad Press for bringing this book back to life. Thanks to Greg F. Gifune for being the first to read SIN all those years ago, and to Shane Ryan Staley for doing the original formatting and design.

PROLOGUE

IN THE BEGINNING

December 16th, 1978

The Star. Mrs. Twining says it means that wishes will come true, that all things dark will disappear. I look at the tarot card again then slip it beneath my pillow. I liked the picture, a pretty girl gazing into a river, so I stole it from Mrs. Twining. She'll never figure it out, she forgets things. People like her are easy to fool. She doesn't remember to take in her laundry, even when it's storming—like now.

Rain thumps against my window and lightning dances across the room—reminds me of the fireworks we saw at the state fair last summer. I'm not scared of thunderstorms. I like them, especially when they come at night.

Today was my tenth birthday. Wish I was older so I could learn to read tarot cards like Mrs. Twining down the hall or wear pretty night clothes like the ladies in the magazines Dad keeps under his bed.

I'm wearing a cotton nightie. There are pink and blue bears on the sleeves and around the neck. Guess I can pretend it's silky and elegant.

There's only one blanket covering me 'cause it's warm tonight. Daddy says it should be colder up here in December.

I hear him talking in the living room. Some men came to see him earlier. They were still here when I kissed him goodnight. One has a scar on his face and he reminds me of the motorcycle guys who hang outside the drugstore. The other guy is dressed in a suit. He looks like James Bond, but he talks like he's from Brooklyn.

James Bond gave me a dollar and patted me on the head. Scarface just ignored me.

They both seemed really interested in Dad's paintings. They tracked mud on the kitchen tile, and dribbles of rainwater from their clothes made spots on the parlor rug. Dad didn't seem to mind though.

The rain is coming down harder and the voices in the other room are lower. There's a sound like beads clicking and it smells like flowers. Feels like the air got thicker; like somebody's in here with me. I see something—right in front of my bed.

There.

I saw him real clear after the last bolt of lightning. He's a black man, but he looks different than the black guys around here. He looks like those African native guys in the old movies on TV or in National Geographic.

My heart is thumping. I want to call my father, but it feels like something's stuck in my throat. I sit up and the card falls from under my pillow. It rises up, spins around and lands in the man's open hand. He smiles at me, not in a scary way. His eyes sparkle, like when Mrs. Twining pins my drawings of her cat to her wall.

The lump in my throat is gone, but something's still not right. The man holds the card between his thumb and forefinger. The pretty girl looks sad and the river has turned red.

"Daddy, Daddy…"

I hear Dad's footsteps. He's here now. His face is serious.

"Sugar plum, what's up? Daddy's sort of busy with the men out there."

"There's somebody standing over there."

"Where?"

"In front of my bed."

He switches on the light. "There's nothing—nobody here, Ruby. You had a dream."

"I saw him. I really did."

He rubs his chin with his thumb. There's blue paint on the tip. He smells of the soap in the upstairs bathroom. "Tell you what. I'll leave your light on, okay?"

I check under my pillow and the card is still there. Of course, it was a dream.

"Okay."

He kisses me on my cheek. "Night, baby."

"Night."

Right after that, I guess I fell asleep, and Dad must've come in later and shut off the light because when I open my eyes it's dark in the room again. The black man is back and standing next to me on the side of my bed. He looks down at me and touches my pillow. There's blood on his hands.

I want to scream and call my Dad but he puts his finger up to his lips like he's saying "Shhh". His eyes are so kind.

Thunder booms and lightning lights up my room again. But he's gone.

The rain lulls me back to sleep.

1

COMING TO NAZARETH

August 2001

I wish it would rain.

Seabirds circle above, wings gliding with the wind, dark angels guarding the Earth below. The sun sinks and slowly disappears behind slate blue clouds.

The salty air smells good. It's been so damn hot. There have been record-breaking temperatures across the Northeast for the past three days. It was reported that on Monday the thermometer rose to one hundred and eight degrees in New York City.

Humid summer nights remind me of a loft I once had in SoHo, where my canvases lined the walls. Painting in mid-August, with fans blowing all around me.

Heat.

Johnny Candelo.

They went hand in hand.

Too bad I hooked up with him—the wrong guy. Too bad the people he double-crossed were the kind who nobody in their right mind dared to fuck with.

Johnny was crazy, no doubt. There's nothing he wouldn't do for money. Lucky for me *they* smoked him and then kindly asked me to leave town.

All in your best interests, they said.

I miss that loft in SoHo.

I miss the sounds of the city, Johnny's smile and the way

he'd watch me as I blended color on my palette. Things were going well in New York. I'd hooked up with a group of other artists and we sold our work on West Broadway.

Wish things had been different back in New York, but I guess I was always meant to be a traveling woman.

Mick Jagger is singing *Ruby Tuesday* on the radio.

Funny both Bo Bo Sims *and* Mrs. Hudson called me that at one time or another.

My first name is Ruby, but my last name has never been Tuesday. I was born Rubina Gianetti back in Denver. My parents had me when they were just kids. Mom left my father when I was a year old. He was just a nineteen-year-old guy alone with a baby, a stable boy for a racehorse owner. He earned minimum wage. My dad always had a certain charm and he fell in with the right people, made some money on the races. I have a sneaking suspicion that a lot of it wasn't legal. But he always took care of me if I needed a hand.

I inherited my artistic talents from my dad. He's used his abilities in some very unique ways over the years.

He told me he was too young when he met my mother, didn't know his *real* self, but a guy over at the stables took the time to make him realize just *who* he really was—taught him well. Me and my pop, we have an understanding. I respect his lifestyle and he respects mine.

I quit school at sixteen. I was smart enough, got good grades, but was bored easily. English was okay. I loved Shakespeare and The Canterbury Tales. My guidance counselor cut art from my schedule; said I needed more discipline and it was his way of handling it. Claimed a more rigid workload would keep me out of trouble. It didn't work.

What trouble? I conned Suzy Bentley into giving me her school lunch money every day. Told her I'd get her a date with Angelo Mendesa; wasn't my fault if she believed my bull. I got Harry Dillon to do my English term paper too. He thought he'd get a date with *me*. Both of them talked too much. Can't blame them, they were just kids and I was a cheat.

I worked odd jobs for a couple years after I left school. I waited tables, cleaned houses, and tended bar. Last job I had was at a club in downtown Denver. A regular named Dr. Armand Stadler took a shining to me. He was in his forties, quite handsome and eager to get his hands up my skirt. He ran a New Age shop in town. He'd published some books on astrology and fortune telling.

He talked real smooth, had lots of money. He got to my heart and I gave in to him. Tables turned, he was my first.

I always believed that nobody gets anything for nothing, so I picked his brain, had him teach me to read the tarot, about herbal magic and how to get people so hooked on the occult that they'd return week after week—sometimes day after day—for readings and spells.

When I was eighteen I up and left the Rocky Mountains. Dad kissed me and told me to call him if I ever got in a jam.

Armand put a curse on me. "By the power of water, earth, fire, and air you'll never find lasting love." He was calm, sitting on his sofa, cup of tea in hand, probably thinking he'd scared me into staying. "Never," he screamed when I walked away.

Changed my name to Ruby Gia when I got over the state border. Since then I've used several variations of my original name.

Lately, I've been Ruby Nicholas.

Nicholas was my Dad's first name at birth. He's changed it a few times as well—along with many other aspects of his life. I also get my freedom-loving spirit from my father.

Now Mick is singing the part about being free. As far as I'm concerned it *is* the only way to be. Freedom is priceless. Nobody asking where I'm going, where I've been or breathing over my shoulder every time I make a move.

You'll never find lasting love.

Even in this weather, there's nothing like the free life.

Freedom. Isn't that what it's all about?

I think of all those people who get up each morning, go to air-conditioned offices and spend the best part of the day hunched over a computer. What kind of life is that?

Not me.

Not Ruby.

I've got my sweet Matty. I've got my potions. My tarot

deck. I've got some canvases stashed in the back of my van—some finished, others in various stages of completion. If you look hard enough you can find my art hanging here and there across the country. People like it. Have paid me money for it. One day—maybe when I'm too old for this life—after I've saved up enough bread—I'm gonna open a gallery. Maybe I'll go back to Manhattan and exhibit the street artists who the upper-class galleries snub. It's not easy standing on the pavement in the boiling sun, waiting for a sale, or just a pat on the back from an admirer. Once, on a hot day like this, a gallery director threw a pan of water at us. She said it was "to cool things off", but the bitch just wanted us off the sidewalk. She ruined two of my watercolors and an Armani blouse I'd lifted out of a boutique on Madison the night before.

Things can be tough, whether it's selling art to tourists on the street, or hustling spells to old women. The best of us just roll with the punches. The weak settle way before their time.

I'm glad I'm away from Boston. It was hotter than any New York City summer I remember—in more ways than one. The college kids have all gone home. And most of the old rich ladies who came from Newton, for readings and for my *remedies,* would rather sit home in their air-conditioned mansions. Or spend their time stalking Laurie Cabot's shop in Salem.

I'm heading straight down to Atlantic City. My connection is there, will be for a while. Lots of opportunities for a girl like me. Men are weak. They gamble. Get drunk. A pretty girl can make a mint. That's what I've been told—and that's what I've learned.

Women are eager to know the future. To possess the magic to change things that aren't quite right.

To hell with Boston and a landlord who gets ticked when I can't pay the rent on time. He didn't supply AC. Sleeping in that damn hole was near impossible for the past few days. To hell with the cops asking all those questions about Mrs. Hudson. Things were getting too sticky. So what if they told me to stay put until everything was settled?

Settled isn't a word in my vocabulary. While I've still got this body—this face—and while I can still talk the talk—I'm a traveling woman.

I'm just a false shaman, claiming to have magical powers—ancient wisdom. Oh sure, I see things sometimes—have these dreams—stuff that's happened since I was a kid. No big deal. My father told me it happens to everybody. Most people ignore it. Others have snatches of it happening through their whole lives and never do anything about it.

Dad said it's the wise person who learns to *listen.*

I'm not so good at listening.

The stuff I make up during my readings and the spells I create are the things that make me money—the fake stuff.

Real to me is when some old broad is handing me a wad of twenties for saying that her old boyfriend from the 1950s is coming back into her life.

I've been so many places.

I've gotten tired of some. Other times circumstances have driven me to leave.

Got booted out of Thorn Bush, Georgia for scamming the local housewives. Me and a partner had a nice tidy business set up there. Wasn't our fault if they believed rosemary and lilac sewed into a pouch and worn inside their bras would make them sexier. They paid me fifty bucks for that stuff.

I smile as I gaze into my rear-view mirror. Now my old wooden box sits in between suitcases and my other belongings. It's filled with rosemary, violet, roots, and thorns—ingredients guaranteed to cure arthritis, bring back lost love, and grant protection from enemies.

Those Southern ladies even believed me when I told several of them there was a curse on their families. They needed to come back six times before the evil went away. I swore them all to secrecy. My partner said I went too far over the top with that one. That sooner or later things would catch up with me.

I told him he was overreacting.

Then I had one of my dreams about Johnny. He was in a frenzy—the way he used to get when he lost a bet or when somebody cheated him out of money. He was pulling my bags out of my bedroom closet, piling my clothes and belongings next to me.

You got to leave town, kiddo.

Leave as quick as you can.

Then he winked and I saw a vision of the village women. They were in single file, walking right through my bedroom. Johnny was watching them, arms folded. Some had knives, others had hatchets.

Don't worry about asking your partner for your share of the profits before you hit the highway—cause even if ya don't, Karma will bring you back together to settle the score.

Johnny waved his arms as the Southern ladies walked through him. They rushed at me, dozens of them—then stopped short a few feet away from me and began to stab and mutilate each other.

These are damn evil bitches, Ruby—up to more harm than you, me or your damn partner could ever conjure.

Run.

It sucked when a bunch of them got together one afternoon for lunch. They drank too much wine. They confided in each other. They came to the conclusion that it was more than coincidence that a dozen families in one small town were all plagued by the same curse. All of them paying the same lady a hundred dollars a pop to be curse-free.

Didn't seem fair that my partner made off with most of the profits before I could gather my stuff and split. But what did Johnny say about Karma and evening things up?

A couple weeks later when I was spending some time in Virginia, just taking a coffee break, I bought a newspaper and read that some women from Thorn Bush, Georgia had gone on a rampage, murdered their husbands and then hacked each other to death. Seems they were into some sort of heebie-jeebie crap that one of them learned in New Orleans—*bad Voodoo.*

I thanked Johnny for watching over me as I drank bitter coffee from the local diner. I saw his face in the dark liquid when I put my cup back on the saucer. He was winking—just like in the dream.

I ignored the dreams at first, turned away from the visions. I don't like dealing with them, but Johnny was persistent, kept haunting me until I paid some attention.

Figuring out the dreams was tough at first, like putting together the pieces of a David Lynch flick. I had to watch *Lost Highway* a few times before it all fell into place. Trouble with dreams is that you can't rewind them and you can't pop one back into the VCR the following night. I'm getting better at it now, but sometimes it still takes me a while. Proves I'm not very good at that kind of thing. I'm better at talking a slick talk.

I pass a restaurant with a billboard outside saying they serve *real* Buffalo wings and cold draft beer. I'd stop, but the place looks a bit unkempt. Besides this is New England, known for lobster, clam chowder and some of the best Italian dishes in the states. I lick my lips. My stomach rumbles. Last thing I ate was a bag of chips, washed down with a cup of coffee. That was six this morning. Man, authentic Buffalo wings and pizza would taste good right now.

The wings and pizza are the best in upstate New York.

I had some really good times there—some bad ones too.

In Buffalo, I hooked up with a guy named Bo Bo Sims. He spotted me one night when I was reading tarot cards at a sleazy bar thirty minutes from Niagara Falls. He said a girl like me could go far. He'd get me into show business. He was a professional wrestler and a promoter. Did those big extravagant shows where ongoing feuds spark fans into attending match after match, as the tension builds between the two behemoths. I was Bo Bo's valet. I led him onto the stage dressed in spandex and sequins. He said we'd get a movie deal before long. He was talking to some guys about it.

This was the late eighties. I was twenty—just a kid. Wrestling was getting big. That dude Vince McMahon was paving the way with pay-per-view TV, even had a WrestleMania at the convention center in Atlantic City.

Bo Bo said he had it all under control. We were going places fast. He made lots of money on advance tickets for shows scheduled far into the nineties.

It was all bullshit.

One night he told me he had no intention of putting on those shows. He opened his safe. My eyes almost popped out of my head when I saw all the cash he'd stowed away. He was planning on going to the West Coast.

I told him I had other plans.

He gave me ten thousand bucks. Later I used it for bail money when I got into a scrape in Dallas.

He still had plenty of money for himself.

Plenty.

He stashed a half million inside the linings of some capes and jackets he used to wear in the ring. He packed them and put a few hundred in a briefcase.

"Never can be too careful," he said, then he wished me luck.

My connection told me that Bo Bo had some trouble before he got out of town. A few guys who he owed protection money to got him in the airport parking lot. They beat him up pretty bad. Took the briefcase. Ripped open his suitcases. When they didn't find anything of value they flattened all the tires on his '86 Camaro and made bad jokes about his wrestling gear.

Little did they know.

Connection also said that Bo Bo was promoting again—wrestling, boxing. Places like Philly. Newark. Baltimore. He also had his hand in a couple of strip joints over in Camden.

Connection said he still talked about me. Bo Bo was a kid's fantasy, a ticket backstage where some of the sexiest and hottest wrestlers congregated. Little did he know, once or twice, behind his back, I got a little extra loving. I was star struck back then. What can I say?

I've known too many like Bo Bo over the years.

The years. They go by like flashes. Blink like the signs you pass on the highway. They're quick and hopeful welcomes to cities and towns—and much quicker exits when things go wrong.

Had to leave New Mexico when the wife of a local businessman hired that private detective. The businessman liked young blondes. He loved having his fortune told in a hot tub. He paid by the hour. Hey, his wife gave me two grand to get lost.

I'm no fool.

It's easy to hook the young ones, the old ones, the middle-aged men who are trying to regain their youth, the desperate and lonely.

Yeah, Atlantic City looked really good when I jumped in my old beat-up van and started driving. But forty miles out of Providence the scenery changed. The trees were greener. There were more of them. And a sign that announced *Beaches* caught my eye.

Now I'm traveling down a winding road. The ocean is in sight. I smell steamers and chowder cooking. Girls in cutoffs and halter tops strut down the street. A neon sign flashes ahead. *Bristo's.* A string of small motels and gift shops line the street.

Another sign welcomes me to Nazareth. Population 2,300. It's an old fishing town with charm. One of those quaint places where city folks come to find refuge in the midst of summer.

Matty, my Maine Coon, stretches in the passenger's seat. He lifts his head and sniffs. He looks at me and lets out a *meow* of approval.

"A bowl of chowder would be nice. Some real New England clam cakes and a bottle of beer would hit the spot before we head out again."

Maybe.

Matty sits up. Arches his back.

I reach over to rub his head. "And a bowl of milk and some tuna for you."

He purrs. Such a good cat. Loves to travel by car. Stays by my side when I walk or prances a few feet ahead, gazing back from time to time to reassure himself that I'm still there. Odd for a feline to say the least. Lucky for me.

A card reader—*an authentic one*—once told me that I'd lived many times before.

A feline soulmate. That's what Matty is. A little spark of energy left over from another lifetime. A part of my own old soul, or of someone who I once loved dearly— from ancient Egypt or from deep in a cave at Lascaux, where—on rock walls—I painted the wild animals I'd hunted—a spirit manifested in that furry body, to accompany me in this life's journey.

Now Mick is belting out *Gimme Shelter.* The DJ just said he's doing a block of the Rolling Stones.

I wish they'd do some Stevie Nicks. A client once told me I

reminded him of Stevie a bit. It was a compliment. I've always loved her music.

I spot an empty cottage. There's a *For Rent* sign on the lawn. Red, yellow, and pink rose vines stretch across a sagging porch. Squirrels and blue jays run and dive across the yard. There's a small apple tree to the right of the house. I wonder if the fruit is good—no matter, I won't be here when it's apple-picking time. The windows need cleaning and the grass needs to be cut, but that's okay.

Looks inviting. A haven from the madness, but for how long?

Settle?

Maybe for a while, I think, as I watch a group of elderly women make their way out of a shop. A sign above the door says the shop's name is Pearl Bones. Strange. When I lived in Georgia, my partner had a collie with that name. The dog was old. Died of cancer. We both cried for weeks.

On the shop window, it says *Help Wanted*. People file out of the shop's door. One woman holds a crystal, stretching her arm as far as she can, moving the stone slowly back and forth like it's something special, like there's some kind of miracle inside. Another turns to gaze at prints of moons, suns, and stars in the shop window.

Inside the store, I catch a glimpse of the owner.

I know him.

Dean Pearson. Con artist. One of the best. Once a promising screenwriter and director. He made some bad deals. Some actors screwed him. Somebody else ripped off an entire screenplay from him. The name of it was *Zombies of the Bayou*. He let me read the manuscript— damn good if you like tales of the undead. I saw the stolen version advertised on cable last year. I heard they plan to do a sequel this fall. Too bad Dean got the short end of the deal and ended up losing a ton of cash.

Funny how people end up.

Weird how things work out.

I can't believe he's here.

The son-of-a-bitch.

This is all coming together too easily.

Karma.

I slow down. Pull over to the curb. He counts cash. He smiles as he shuts his register and dims the lights. He lights a cigarette as night cloaks this city by the sea in deep purples and blues and the shadows grow darker, making silent mysteries of what daylight shows off.

Our eyes meet, color drains from his face.

I drive away.

Tomorrow I'll pay him a visit.

I pass an old Victorian house badly in need of a paint job. It's dark inside. A sagging porch with a broken railing plays host to several men and a woman.

I gaze at a full moon, white and glaring like a harlot in a stygian sky, sprinkled with perfect, shining stars. I think of Mrs. Hudson and her money tucked away safely with my herbs, roots, and a collection of knives my father bought me in Canada. I reach down, slip my hand inside my boot. My favorite knife is long and sharp, there for emergencies.

Nazareth. The cost of living is lower here—the prospects just as good as Atlantic City at this time of year.

"Perfect," I sigh as I think about the cottage. I'll inquire about it in the morning. Tonight, Matty and I will sleep on the beach. It'll be too hot and crowded in the van and I'm not about to pay an inflated motel bill.

I turn around and swing into *Bristo's* parking lot.

A young girl and a guy who looks to be in his late thirties, seem to be arguing by a truck parked in the lot. The man is handsome, rugged, with dark hair. Italian looking—a hint of Spanish. Like so many of the natives here. The girl is tattooed, thin—too thin—with straight blonde hair and pale skin. They stare at me as I pass by. My long skirt catches the wind. Silver jewelry jingles. My feline walks beside me. It's second nature to him. His green eyes reflect lights.

At the take-out window, I ask for clam cakes, chowder, and a glass of beer for myself. I order a bowl of milk and tuna in a plastic cup for Matty.

I take a seat at a table on the wooden deck. I watch my cat lap at milk. His eyes are closed in elation. His bushy tail flicks back and forth.

I enjoy the small lush meal before me. Tastes of fish, salt, cream, and tangy fried batter. Man, I was hungry. It's not Buffalo wings and pizza, but just as good.

The man and girl continue to argue. Their voices rise and fall with the ocean waves. The man jerks a canvas bag out of the girl's hand, dumps its contents on the ground and reaches down to pick up a leather pouch. He pulls the drawstrings, wets a finger and plunges it into the pouch. He brings his finger to his lips, then shakes his head. He grabs the girl by her hair, opens the passenger side of the truck and shoves her inside.

I hear her scream. His voice overpowers her cries.

The girl's canvas bag and its contents remain on the ground—something round and shiny, perhaps a mirror, a pack of cigarettes, a notebook and what looks like a dozen or more tubes of lipstick are also left behind. He tosses the pouch inside the truck.

The man gets into the driver's side. Engine roars. They drive past me. Sand and dust erupt from the wheels. She runs her finger over the window. Looks at me. Terror is in her eyes.

A domestic squabble I don't want any part of. Maybe a father and daughter. Maybe lovers. Who can tell these days? People think they're settling into a nice comfortable life, but there are always problems. Fights. Differences. It's better to be free.

I finish my meal and stroke Matty who has also finished and is settled into the comfortable fabrics on my lap. I gaze at the stars. What would they tell me if I could really read them? Am I making the right choice? Do I ever?

I hear Johnny's voice. It's coming from somewhere deep inside my brain. Or is it my heart?

Settling ain't in your blood.

The spell of Nazareth isn't meant to last.

Matty looks up at me with wide eyes. Did he hear the same voice?

He closes his eyes and then reopens them slowly like cats do when they're sort of smiling at their human companions, then he settles deeper into the folds of my skirt.

I've been sitting here enjoying the night. About a half-hour has passed. The truck turns back into the lot. The man is alone now. He walks past me as he makes his way to the take-out window. He orders a beer.

He sits with an elderly black man at a table a few feet away. They speak softly. The old man gazes at the stars and makes circles in the air with his index finger. I hear him say something about the wind, phases of the moon.

The younger man sees me staring. I'm obvious most times. Can't help it. Curious like a cat. He nods. Those eyes. They try to hold my attention. They have no power over me. Men lost the ability to hold me—with a look, with words, with feelings—years ago. He's good-looking enough, but I don't get involved. Can't. I won't be here long enough.

I stroke silky fur. Hum a song by Stevie Nicks. Feel good as the breeze strokes my face.

He must have taken my curious stare as a sign of flirtation because now he's making his way over here. I hear soft chuckles from the old man.

He stops in front of me. Looks at my cat. At the rings on my fingers. Then at my van.

On closer inspection, I notice that his dark hair has a soft reddish tinge to it. It's a bit long, just touching his shoulders. He's wearing a small gold earring in his left ear. No rings, just a simple Timex watch. His dark eyes have specks of green in them. Devilish eyes. The kind that must drive most women crazy. Not me though. He's wearing cutoff jeans with threads hanging off the ends. His shirt is a University of Rhode Island pullover. His sandals look new; good leather.

"New York plates. New in town? Tourist?" His voice is gruff. New England clipped speech. Macho attitude.

"What's it to you?"

Matty hisses.

"I lived here since I was born. Know everybody. The same tourists come back here year after year. You aren't one of them."

His tone is condescending. His macho stance amuses me. "Am I under arrest? Under suspicion? Are you a cop?"

He laughs. Rich. Deep. "You're very pretty. I—never mind." He thinks a minute. Then speaks. "I'm Michael Elmira."

I sense something else in his tone. His eyes. I know he really isn't grilling me, he's just a guy trying to score. This is his reality check. All that macho stuff is fine for young girls in trouble and old men who long for youth, but not for the stranger who just blew into town.

He looks lost for words. I sense sadness, loneliness.

I soften. "My name is Ruby Nicholas. I just moved from Boston. Looking for a place for the summer—maybe longer—don't know."

"There's a cottage a few blocks down."

"Yeah, I saw it."

"I own it."

"Do you allow pets?"

"Do you have references?"

"There's a guy I worked for. He's down in Jersey now—for the summer. I could give you his name."

"What kind of work did you do?"

"Housecleaning." I want to burst out laughing, but I remain cool. "I'm an artist. I needed another job to pay the bills—to put some money away so I could take the summer off to paint and make little gift things, you know." Best not to tell all. That's all he needs to know.

"Artist type, huh? I know a few of them already." He slides a napkin across the table. "Got a pen?"

I do. I reach into my bag.

My heart does a few extra thumps as I write the name and number. I gotta make a call before he does. My man in Jersey is slick. We'll pull it off.

He gives me that macho stare. My own steady gaze reminds him that it doesn't work with me. He makes a move to pet Matty. The cat growls deep and low. "Last guy who lived there had two Dobermans. A kitty cat won't be a problem."

He hands me a card. Name. Phone number.

He takes a deep breath. He's redeemed himself as far as he's concerned. Little does he know.

"Meet you there at noon."

I nod my head.

He walks back to his table. A group of people has stopped

there, two women and two men. They chat with the old man. They all look up and smile as Michael approaches.

The owner of *Bristo's*—a stocky balding man—tells me that my van will be okay parked there all night. People do it all the time. He'll be in the back room playing poker anyway.

I collect my things and stroll off to the beach.

I make a quick call to Jersey. "I'm going to be late. I'm safe. Still have most of the money you sent me. You know me," I say. "I think I can score here—besides I need a break after that Mrs. Hudson incident. And, oh, by the way, there'll be a call coming in to you…"

The voice on the other end of the line is reassuring. It's OK. I can have all the time I need. My ass is covered.

There's a newsstand by the phone booth. The headlines scream about another victim of the Ocean State Murders. People were buzzing about it in Boston. Was even on the national news a couple of times. There's always one serial killer or another causing havoc. They come and go in this country—like the music of the times—or movies. We had disco and The Son of Sam going on at the same time—Charles Manson and The Doors. Just good old American pop culture.

I purchase a paper from the grumpy old vendor. I sit on an empty bench. Matty snuggles close as he watches seabirds swoop above.

The story says that the victim was an artist—blonde—pretty—just like all the others. The third victim this summer in Southern Rhode Island. All the murders took place at night. The victims were all murdered in their homes; either stabbed or shot with a .44 Magnum.

Well, I'm sleeping on the beach tonight. My companion is a cat who growls and attacks like a banshee when he's threatened. I've got a knife in my boot and the last man who tried to fuck with me lost his right thumb.

Besides, an unmarked detective's car has circled at least once every ten minutes since I've been here. I'm sure he's watching for kids with drugs, drunks and the like. There are also two squad cars parked outside the donut shop across the way. They're not moving. Won't be all night.

Beneath the early August moonscape, I spread my quilt made of shades of blue. I nestle close to my purring feline. Feel his whiskers brush my cheek. Know he knows more about the universe, its scents, what lies in its secret crevices, than any fake shaman.

I wish I could scoop up tonight's sky with all its twinkling stars and pretty moon. I lift my hands and open my palms as if to draw on its beauty.

My bracelets click together. I wear two silver bands, etched with Egyptian cats on my right wrist. I wear three silver chains with Art Noveau cat charms on my left wrist. I stole them all when I was eight, one by one from a gift shop in Florida.

Dad was there on business. He was nervous, edgy, the way he always gets when a deal starts to come together.

He booked a room at a small hotel on Biscayne Boulevard in Miami. He knew the woman at the registration desk, called her by her first name—Elita. He smiled and waved at guests who sat by the pool, or who read newspapers in the lobby. He seemed to know everybody.

Every day after lunch Elita would come to our room. She'd baby-sit me while my father went to meetings. She was bone thin and chewed a lot of gum. Dad said she was a friend and owed him a favor.

The routine was the same each day. Elita would look at me with red-rimmed eyes, then she'd rummage through her purse. "Trying to quit smoking," she'd tell me. "The gum helps. Do me a bitty favor and go down to the hotel shop and get more." She'd hand me a couple bucks. "Get some candy for yourself. We'll go sit by the pool when you get back."

At a dusty, damp-smelling gift shop I first spotted my bracelets hanging on a display rack on the counter. The cats on the silver bands winked at me. The felines on the silver chains told me they wanted to go home to Denver with me. I knew I had to obey their wishes, even if I'd only imagined them.

A few years before that my father had read me a story about silver cats on a fairy queen's bracelets, said they came alive when she danced in little girls' dreams. That story enchanted me and I felt that *those* bracelets were there just for me.

There was a school kid minding the shop, one who never paid much attention to what was going on, so it was easy for me.

The jewelry didn't fit me until I was around thirteen, but I loved it and held it sacred until then. I still do today. Reminds me so much of my dad.

I hug Matty, and the charms make soft tinkling noises.

I hear singing, talking and some laughter.

There are people on the beach—the four who were with Michael over at *Bristo's*. They look so carefree in their faded shirts and worn-out shorts. They all look magical and filled with mischief. I like that look. Reminds me of a lot of folks I've known. There's a blonde woman and another woman with hair so black that the moonlight turns it deep blue. There's also a dark-skinned man—mulatto—and another man with curly red hair. They're all wearing shorts and thin shirts. All are barefooted. They beat small drums hanging from ropes around their necks. First slow and soft. Then hard and quick. Their voices ring above the drumbeats.

They make a circle.

Chanting.

Hands move so quickly that they become a blur. Four pairs of eyes gaze at a lush moon. Voices blend with the sea's lullaby. They dance round and round. Faster and faster, until there is a frenzy of music, enchantment, and water splashing as waves roll in. I delight in the sensuous, energetic bodies weaving, jumping, celebrating the night.

Suddenly they stop. They break into laughter, slapping each other playfully.

The dark-skinned man speaks, but some of his words disappear as the waves crash the shore. "...made a clean thousand...house on the East Side of Providence...cased the place for three days straight..."

Thieves. Con men. I feel at home already.

The blonde woman spots me. She smiles. "Hey lady, we saw you talking with Michael—*Baba* Michael". She comes closer, smiling. Her hips are wide and her pretty face is plump and dimpled. There are scars on her arms and on her wrists. She smells of lemon and the sea.

The dark-haired woman smiles at me. Her black mascara is smudged. She bends down to pet Matty. "We'll see you soon."

They sing as they walk away, lulling me to sleep. I dream about Nazareth, Michael Elmira, people dancing on a beach where the stars shine down like guardian angels. I see the lights in Atlantic City and vermilion streams on pale white skin. I see the end of the world.

Then Johnny comes, takes my hand and we walk on the beach. He shows me things—always does.

I'm back in New York City, dreaming of a mystery man. Not Johnny. Just the shadowy man who shows up during sleep every now and then. I see him move, talk— live—like I'm watching a movie. Like he's this incredible actor.

It's 1997.

He's watching me from a sidewalk cafe across the street from where I'm leaning my canvases against a boarded up storefront

What a beautiful woman.

His words float to me like a soft lullaby.

Now, I'm watching two men, listening to them. The images become clearer—words ring out like the chimes at Saint Paul's in lower Manhattan.

The man's friend sips his coffee and laughs. "She's just one of the street artists here. One of the ones we consistently chase away and on occasion have to arrest."

"For selling art? In SoHo? You've got to be kidding."

"Mayor's orders."

"Are you going to stop her now? What's the harm?" They watch me as people stop to admire my work.

The friend speaks again. "No harm, if you ask me. The mayor is at war with these people. He believes that visual artists don't have first amendment rights like writers—or politicians. It's all part of his program to clean up the city. Besides local merchants complain that the artists distract the public from buying their stuff."

"Christ, she's in front of a string of deserted stores."

"That's why I only see a lovely blonde. She's smiling—and what a glorious smile—and just talking to passersby."

The scene fades away and I hear the man whisper:

She's here now. I'm sure of it.

Colors blur. Shadows retreat between alley-ways and beneath the feet of those who walk the night while other souls sleep.

And I drift away again. Tomorrow night I'll have a bed to dream in.

2

THE FIRST DAY

I awaken to seabirds screaming. Matty is hunched next to me and looking up at them, making soft clicking noises and twitching his nose.

"Forget it, buster, those seagulls are bad news. If you bit into one of them you'd be sorry."

Meow.

"Okay, let's get you settled and then I need a shower."

There's a shower and changing area a few feet away. I'll clean up and change there, but first I take Matty back to the van, pour him a bowl of dry food, fill his water dish and change the litter in his box. I find some clean clothes; cool cotton pants, an embroidered shirt and silver sandals.

I'll keep my knife in my pocket.

The shower feels good. I'll let my hair dry naturally. It'll take a few hours, but in the end, it'll hang in soft ringlets around my face and down my back.

I check on Matty and see that he's settled into the driver's seat, ears perked up, eyes half-closed. He doesn't want to be bothered with people things right now. He's off somewhere in a cat dream. I'll respect that. I crack the window open for him. It'll be getting hotter later on and I don't want to leave him there for too long.

I have some breakfast at *Bristo's;* coffee, a cranberry muffin, and a bag of salt and vinegar chips. I read the morning paper and anticipate my meeting with Mr. Elmira. I turn to the horoscope page, look at the daily predictions for the sign Sagittarius and laugh as I read. It says, *You are about to encounter a new beginning, but beware of unseen forces. Be careful who you trust.*

That's the story of my life in a nutshell.

"Nothing like cash to make things nice and tidy," Michael Elmira says, counting the money. His teeth are white. Straight. Contrast his tanned skin. He's dressed in jeans today. A dark short-sleeved pullover shows off his toned muscles. The green specks in his eyes seem to sparkle. He knows I'm checking him out. He knows he's hot looking. He throws back his shoulders, smiles slow and sexy. Okay, I admit it, he's starting to charm me—a lot.

"Keep the place clean and the noise to a minimum. Rent's due again a month from today."

"Deal," I say, thinking a month may be all I need in Nazareth. I sense that he doesn't want to leave, that he'll keep talking if I encourage it.

I notice the girl is sitting in his truck. Still. Silent. Like a wisp of white.

"Daughter?"

"That's my niece, Gracie. Her mother's in prison. I'm her legal guardian for now. She's a *problem*—just like her mother. I've got some friends on the force. I brought her to the station down the road last night. Gave her a chance to chill out in a juvenile cell. She had coke and heroin in her bag—running through her veins too. I'm taking her to rehab up in Providence today." He looks to his truck.

"You live close by?"

"I have a house up the road. I call it Green Briar. My great grandfather bought it for a song during the depression. After my parents died, his money and the house got passed down to me." He chuckles slightly. "Lots of stories surrounding the house and its past. Colorful stuff. I don't know if I really believe any of it, but occasionally you hear a bump in the night."

"I know the house. I saw a bunch of people—"

"It offers shelter to what others view as the underbelly of society. People have come and gone from there over the years. Some have remained. They're welcome to stay forever if they want. All I ask is that they help out with food, any work that needs to be done, and the basics of life."

"Some people have rotten luck."

"Yeah. Tough breaks." He shakes his head. "I've opened my doors to people who need shelter. Some are dealing with massive problems. Others have had tough breaks in life." He looks thoughtful for a moment then says, "I teach English in town during the school year, by the way."

"Respectful employment," I say.

He smiles. "My niece will be eighteen in a month. She's threatening to go on her own. There's nothing I can do to stop her. I don't want to think about what lies ahead for her." He sighs. "I'll have to try my best to do what I can for her now." He looks to his truck again. "I've got things to do. Best I leave."

Something lingers in the air. In his eyes. A charge of electricity zigzags through my heart.

Attraction.

I don't need this—not now.

I smile the smile that some people have said is incredible. An asset I've learned to use when I can't think of the right thing to say, or when what I'm about to say may not be right. "Thanks for giving me shelter."

He nods and walks away, slipping the money into his pocket. Mrs. Hudson's money. She always said I could do magic with her cash.

I bring my things in from the van, put clean sheets on the bed, a lace cloth on the kitchen table and I hang one of my paintings over the living room couch. The canvas is a scene from my loft window in New York; it's night and the sky is a deep blue. The streets are empty. There is a coffee shop across the street and people are gathered at the counter—young people with dreams, their faces bright and hopeful. My own likeness is in the midst of these people, a cup of coffee before me, my hand resting on the shoulder of a handsome man at my side.

Johnny Candelo.

New York City.

Did I mention that I miss it?

Matty surveys each room—from the small bedroom complete

with a queen-sized bed, a night stand, and a small closet—to the small living room where there is a couch, a wicker rocking chair, and a matching wicker coffee table—then on to a tiny kitchen with a small table, two chairs, and a smaller pantry off to one side. There's a small bath with a shower off to the other side. The floors are hardwood and highly polished. My cat spends a few seconds stretched across the cool surface. Eventually, he takes a spot on the window ledge in the bedroom, watching seabirds sail across the sky.

Thank goodness there's a fan stored in the bedroom closet. I plug it in, put it on high as I change into shorts and a cool cotton shirt.

The knife. I slip it inside my purse. It's time to pay Dean a visit.

I tell Matty I'll be back later, leave him some water and a can of moist food, then walk back out into the hot August sun.

3

PEARL BONES

Silver chimes jingle as I step into Pearl Bones. I quietly remove the *Help Wanted* sign from the door. Angels and fairies smile down at me from colorful greeting cards and posters. An array of sculptures dazzles me—all glimpses of Camelot—a castle—Lancelot—a white stallion. There's also a display of African objects. There are drums, similar to the ones used last night on the beach. There are colorful rattles and maracas and beautiful beaded necklaces. Incense burns. Candles glow on counters. The proprietor is slouched over a table. "If you want a reading I'll be with you in a minute. If not, feel free to look around."

A deck of tarot cards is before him. He turns one over. The Ace of Swords.

"Dean, that's a fucked up reading if I ever saw one." He looks up, startled.

"Jesus, Ruby, what the hell are you doing in Nazareth?"

"I was on my way to Jersey. Saw your sign. Rented a cottage. Now I need a job."

Dean's hair is longer and stringier than ever. There's some gray at his temples and crow's feet are forming around his eyes. He's too thin. His black suit hangs off him like it's five sizes too big. He looks old.

"Geez, Dean, you look like one of those undead characters from the B-films you used to do. Don't you ever eat?"

His eyes water. He laughs shrill and high. "I eat a lot." He points to a bag of chocolate chip cookies on the table. "I can see you haven't changed. Yeah, I can use somebody like you here—besides I owe you one."

I nod my head. "You gonna pay me what you stiffed me out of when we bolted from Georgia?"

"Hey, those hillbillies came after me. They had fucking rifles. I had to run. Besides, I knew you'd take care of yourself." He smiles. He's charming. "I never doubted we'd meet up again—make things right."

"Well, let's make it right then."

"Can you start tomorrow?"

"How about today?"

The door jingles. Two elderly women walk into the shop.

The smallest one speaks. "Any tarot readings today?"

Dean stands to greet them. "Ruby just got back from the Far East with secrets of the soul. She can tell fortunes like nobody else. You must have seen her on TV?"

One woman takes off her glasses. "Yeah…yeah…You were on Oprah."

"I—um—"

"Take a seat, ladies, there's nobody quite like Ruby."

By six—after hearing about countless grandchildren, love affairs gone wrong, money schemes gone bad and one case of herpes—I've taken in a fair amount of money.

Dean stacks neat piles of tens and twenties on the counter. "The stock is selling well to the tourists, but this is more money than I've taken in all week on readings."

"I'm tired. Drove a long way yesterday and slept on the beach. Mind if I quit for today?"

He pats me on the hand. "Stay and eat with me. I ordered Chinese."

"Sure, why not? I'm kinda hungry."

"Glad you came, Ruby. I'll make it all up to you. Ain't got much spare cash lying around right now, but keep today's earnings from the readings. Tomorrow we'll figure out some sort of percentage."

"Look, Dean, we'll do fifty-fifty. Just like the old days. I'm just thankful for this bit of synchronism."

He counts out my share and gently places it into my palm.

A delivery boy carrying several brown paper bags bursts

into the shop. He's small, about 5′6″. A baseball cap shades his large almond eyes. He hands Dean the bags, then smiles wide. "That'll be $12.50, Mr. Dean. The rice has lots of shrimp in it today. I make sure."

Dean gives him a $20 from his share of today's earnings. "Keep the change, Lang."

"Thank you, thank you, Mr. Dean."

Lang spins on his heels and quickly exits.

I feel bad for Dean in a way. I'm such a sucker at times, but him and me go back a long way and he did do me a good turn today.

"Dean, I appreciate the food—everything."

"My pleasure, kiddo."

"I hope I bring you good fortune."

"Just don't start telling people that there's a curse on them and you'll do me just fine."

"Got some dishes and silverware here?"

"Yeah, in the back room. There's a small fridge. Get a bottle of that Chianti too, will ya?"

An elderly woman enters the shop. "Hello, Mrs. Ridley," says Dean. "Your rose sachet is ready. I also got those vanilla candles in that you like. Everything sweet, just like you."

The woman blushes.

I leave Dean alone with his customer. I get the feeling that she'll purchase more than just the sachet.

I'm hungrier than I realized. I fill paper plates with fried rice, chow mein, and shrimp and chicken cooked in thick batter.

We eat slowly, speaking about old times.

"Remember the guy down in Macon who had the hots for you? His family grew tobacco or something like that, didn't they?"

"Yeah, I had him convinced that my ex had stolen all my money and left me for another woman. He'd feel bad whenever I told him I had the blues. So, he'd buy me a gift. It was always something nice—something I could pawn."

"You're such a witch. The guy must have flipped out when you left without a word."

"I left with his wallet and that horrid gold chain he wore."

"Ruby, Ruby, same as always." He looks at his watch, then taps a plastic fork on the edge of his plate. "Want more rice?"

"I'm stuffed. I'll help clean up."

"No, I'll take care of it in a bit."

He gazes towards the street. A young man is leaning against the pole in front of the store. He's dressed in an expensive suit. His dark hair is short and slicked back. He looks at Dean and nods.

Dean's shoulders are hunched. He's sweating, despite the AC. His hands are shaking. He bites his bottom lip thoughtfully. "Hey, look I've got something to tell you."

The man watches us, takes a long drag off his cigarette, quickly flicks it away, then lights another.

"Want to tell me about *him?*"

"That's Joey Gallo. I got some business with him later. He's early. He can wait. There's something else."

"He's not the type who can cause you bodily damage is—"

"Ruby, Joey is a Goodfella wannabee. His family owns a jewelry shop in Providence. I buy those silver unicorn charms from them. I'm working on another project with them. He's just early for our appointment is all. He hasn't a care in the world. He's living in his parent's beach house in Point Judith for the summer. Has plenty of time to kill. Spoiled rotten, the bastard."

"What have you got to say to me then?"

"Back in Georgia, I realized I had no one else in the world—nobody that meant a damn—nobody I could trust." He bites his lip again. "You always had your father. My parents died when I was a kid. No siblings. For me, it was just you. You were the world. A kid sister I never had."

"Yeah, I meant so much that you bailed when trouble brewed."

He ignores my sarcasm. "I had a few grand stashed away back then. I knew I wanted to settle, maybe start a business. I was tired of running. Tired of hustling. Things were a bit unsettled in certain areas of my life, though, and I needed to know that my affairs would be in order in case I got smoked."

I think of Johnny.

"I'm not surprised, but exactly who was after your ass?"

"Tommy Izzi for one. He thought I cheated in a poker game we had on Long Island. Tony Almond wanted me because he claimed I sold him a fake emerald."

"You *did* cheat at cards and you *did* sell fake jewels. What's your point?"

"Both guys were after me, had contacts all over the country on the lookout for me. So, I had a will drawn up—leaving all my worldly possessions to you."

I'm astonished. "I'm sure you've torn it up by now."

"Nope, I still have it. It's still legal. I keep it in the register."

"Those two guys still after you?"

"Both of them got busted. They're serving time. I heard that they're cell mates down in Texas. Isn't that ironic?"

"But you kept the will?"

"Why the hell not? Who else could take over the business—or sell it—if something happens to me? Never know who's gonna come knocking on my door."

"And you knew I'd come to Nazareth?"

"Nazareth, New York, Chicago. People like us are drawn together. You would have found me sooner or later just to even things up. You know you would have—intentionally or by accident—you would have." He touches my hand. "We'll always be two shamans who don't know how to direct our talents—but I think that's the connection we got."

I give Dean a peck on the cheek. "See you at ten tomorrow."

"Hey, bring some of your paintings too. We'll put them in the window. They'll brighten things up."

"Thanks. You sure it's okay with that guy out there?"

"Don't worry. I'll see you later."

I close the door behind me.

Joey smiles. He is rather good-looking despite the wise guy getup. "Afternoon, Miss." I smile my smile and he makes his way through the shop door. He and Dean shake hands. I don't want to stare. Whatever Dean is doing is none of my concern. I got my own demons to wrestle with.

4

MICHAEL THE SANTERO

There's a slight breeze. Street vendors are set up along the street. Some sell flowers. Others display books and bright tapestries. Artists sell their wares. Tourists stop to watch them work, paint, and draw. There are fortune tellers here and there as well. Nobody pays them any mind. I guess my charm is what draws customers to me.

One woman, old and gray-haired, sits by a wooden crate, shuffling cards. She's wearing a black dress and high-laced black boots—like my granny used to wear. She's even got a pair of rosaries hanging out of her pocket. She watches me as I approach.

She's got incense, flowers, fruit, and packets of herbs lined up on her crate. She's got a slight Spanish ring to her voice. "You got more talent than you think, gypsy woman. You pride yourself as a scam artist—but you got better gifts, you just got to get older and wiser."

"That so, old woman?"

She hands me an apple. "*Shango*' is your god. This is an offering to him. He brings passion. Sometimes it's volatile. He's not soft and subtle like all them goddesses of love you always hear about. He comes with the storms. Thunder and lightning. No, nothing tame and sweet for you." She wipes sweat from her forehead with a yellowed embroidered handkerchief, then she puts her elbows on the table and leans over. "You don't know who I am, do you? You will—you will..."

"What are you talking—"

Hands on my shoulders. Michael Elmira's voice. "Lady Lucy. Here's $5 for some lilac and rosemary."

He watches as the woman packages the herbs in plastic baggies. He pays her with five single one dollar bills. She places the baggies in his palm and a flash of the New York skyline flickers through my head. My canvases are lined up against an empty building in SoHo. Was it him who watched me from a distance that day?

"She's a wise one, Michael. Can't fool her, not for one minute."

He looks into my eyes. The old woman's words seem to be still ringing in the humid air. "I can see that. I truly can. Thank you."

He grabs my elbow and leads me away from Lady Lucy's stand. I let him. There's an understanding here. Something quite nice.

I turn for one last look at the women. A nun has stopped at her table. Suddenly the sun is brighter, as if some clouds parted, revealing strong white rays. My eyes water, blurring the scene. Watercolors running together. For a split-second Lady Lucy and the nun melt into each other, becoming one, just an illusion of the light and heat. The nun does the sign of the cross and walks quickly away.

Michael gently tugs at my sleeve. "Out shopping today?"

"No, I actually just started a new job. One of the shops."

"Which one?"

Lady Lucy calls out to us. "You look so lovely together—time will weave such a spell—"

We both laugh.

"She's eccentric at times, but harmless. Just showed up here in June. She told me she traveled here from another realm, that she's an angel." He laughs. "I don't know where she sleeps or stays. People say they've seen and heard her walking the streets and the beach all hours of the night. Poor old soul. I've tried to convince her to come to Green Briar for shelter. She just laughs—every damn time—says angels don't need shelter. But, I have gotten her to come by for meals in the evenings." He looks at me. Smiles. Attraction is forcing its way into our lives. "She always tells me that *Shango'* will find love for me."

"What on Earth is *Shango'*?"

"He's a god. Santeria. Or *La Regla Lucumi* as most of us prefer to call it. *Shango'* is invoked for spells of passion—dominance. He protects those he has an affinity for. He watches over mortals with fiery souls—those who follow their hearts. They say he comes with thunder and lightning. He loves apples, bananas, and roosters."

"Oh, in that order I suppose?"

His mouth twists into a scowl and anger flashes in his eyes. "There are people here who take Santeria very seriously."

"You, for one? Well, tell me more."

The angry look transforms into one of amusement. "What a curious and interesting soul you are. Come, have an iced tea with me. It's too hot to stand out here in the sun. Here, let's sit. I've got to drive out to Warwick later, but I've got a bit of time." He leads me to a sidewalk table, beneath a canopy, outside a small restaurant.

"It's still damn hot," he says as he wipes moisture from his upper lip with a table napkin. His eyes are so beautiful. Almost soulful. I could get lost in them. I'd better not.

The waitress, a middle-aged woman who looks cool and undaunted despite the heat takes our order. She sets the tea in front of us.

"So, do you believe in dreams?"

I don't know why I asked that. Sometimes my mouth reacts before my brain does.

"Everybody has to have beliefs—faith. I studied lots of religions through the years, comparing them and contrasting them with the beliefs I was brought up on. I held on to what I felt was right and discarded what didn't. My father was of Italian descent and my mother Cuban. They met down in Miami in the '50s when he was in the Navy. He was a devout Catholic. She was a bit more creative."

"How so?"

"Her ancestors were typically baptized by the Roman Catholic Church upon their arrival to this country. Their native practices and faiths were suppressed. They developed a unique way of keeping their old religion alive by replacing the gods and goddesses of their traditional religions with the christian saints. For example, *Shango*' is the Catholic Saint Barbara. There's truth in so many of the older religions—things you could not imagine."

I remember the ceremony I'd witnessed on the beach. "I saw some people dancing on the beach last night. They called you *Baba* Michael."

"Max, Linda, and the gang, I presume."

"I didn't get their names. Anyway, you were saying?"

He nods. The green flecks dance. "A *Santero* is a priest. There are different levels of priesthood. A high priest is a *Babalocha. Baba* means father."

"So, the people at Green Briar practice Santeria?"

"People need something to guide them. The people at Green Briar have been through hell and back. They're still trying to figure out what's right and wrong—some still teeter back and forth, but it doesn't matter. They've come to the house because it's the end of the road for them,—it's a safe haven. Some have spent time in the street, often earning money for food by selling their bodies. One man is old and too poor to live the way society dictates. Green Briar isn't for everyone. There's only a handful of people there right now—all regulars. Except for Gracie. She's family and I have a feeling that any day she'll be long gone. I've opened my doors to people who need shelter. Some are dealing with massive problems—have had tough breaks in life." He sips his tea. "I've got to believe. Like I said, we all need a bit of faith to keep us from going astray." He smiles at me. "And in answer to your earlier question—yes, dreams have power. Listen to their messages." He watches as Lady Lucy passes; all her belongings are slung over her shoulder in an ancient sack. "Listen, I may have seen you before— New York—"

Lady Lucy turns to him, "She's the one, Mr. Michael. Summer in SoHo, remember that day?"

The dream I recently had clicks in my head. I'm lost for words so I just say the first thing that pops into my head. "You're a good man, Michael Elmira."

"Nobody is one hundred percent good—or evil."

"Well, you're doing a good thing."

"For the ones who want the help—want to adapt to the lifestyle. I've got to trust in my faith and do the best I can."

Faith.

Magic.

My mind is swirling. Knowledge like this could make me some money down the road. New spells. Magical things people are fascinated with. Hooks to lure in the unsuspecting.

"I'd like to know more."

I'd like to know more about Michael too. He looks into my eyes and then his gaze moves slowly over my body. It gives me the chills.

"I can tell you more, but right now I've got to get out to Warwick," he says as his eyes meet mine once more. "As a matter of fact, there's a ceremony tomorrow night. It's at the house. Come by at eight."

"I'll be there."

"Hey, you never told me what shop you're working at."

"Pearl Bones."

"My, my, what a nice surprise indeed."

"Why?"

"You'll see."

He touches my arm. An image flashes in my head. A silver knife. A heart and stars are etched on its handle. Blood drips from the blade.

Michael smiles. "I went to New York City a few years ago, visited a Botanica on 116th Street, near Park Avenue. Best place I've ever been to in this country for the basic needs of a *Santero*. Lots of the things I'll use in the ceremony were purchased there; candles, beautiful wood carvings of saints, amulets, and talismans. The best find is a sterling silver knife. The etchings on the handle are phenomenal. Done by a Guatemalan artisan. When I use it in a ritual there's always pure magic."

I shiver, but there's no wind on this hot summer day.

5

A MIDSUMMER'S NIGHT DREAM

Tonight, I hear thunder booming in the distance. I wonder if the rain will come. Even with the fan hiked all the way up it's still too damn hot.

Matty is perched on the window ledge, sniffing the night, pressing his head against the screen whenever the wind stirs a bit.

Despite the heat, everything seems to be falling into place. I wonder if I'll be more than friends with Michael. I can't get too attached to him. Yet there's this feeling— this attraction is growing.

Forget about it, girl.

"You're just jealous, Johnny," I say to the night.

How long will it be before I have to leave Nazareth?

My eyes grow heavy. I've left the radio on. It's turned low and the newscaster's voice drones on in monotone. Something about finding another body tonight. A young girl. Blonde. This time the killer stabbed the victim several times before he strangled her to death. She was an artist—just like all the others. She was napping when the killer entered her apartment through an open window.

The girl's body was found in Warwick.

Didn't Michael go out there when he left me? I wonder if he saw anything while he was there.

I think about shutting the window, but I'm too damn tired to move. *You'll be fine,* Johnny's voice floats above me. *Nobody's gonna harm my Ruby tonight—not tonight.* Matty nestles by my side and we drift to sleep as the thunder comes closer.

I hear people chanting, chimes, and drums beating. They're calling my name. They're calling Michael. Laughter. I close my eyes and see Johnny. Blood bubbles from his lips as he tries to speak.

Thunder echoes once more and a distant voice accompanies it. Johnny's voice. *I love you, Cara Mia.*

I dream of a god with dark skin. He has Michael's eyes. He's beating a drum. Thunder claps. Lightning flares above him.

I open my eyes and the drums fade away.

Matty snuggles close.

Now I'm dreaming again, walking with Johnny through Greenwich Village, down Bleeker Street. My canvases are tucked under his arm. He looks down at me and his face is merely a skull. Death. The canvases drip with vermilion and then everything is black and silent.

Ruby.

I wake from sleep. My body is slick with sweat. The alarm clock says it's five in the morning.

I hear a thump outside. A whisper. I think I hear my name again.

I put my robe on, walk through the kitchen and open the door. Nobody's there. Just a stray cat perched on the garbage can.

Upon my doorstep is a cluster of white feathers with peculiar colorful shells around them.

"What the fuck?"

Kids? A prank?

Lady Lucy is picking garbage from a can.

Was she there a moment ago?

She looks up, smiles a toothless smile and waves.

"The Tower," she cries as she limps away. Scarves swirl from her tattered skirt. Her beads click. Her laughter sounds like a witch's cackle. She waves her hands. Feathers float in the air.

Here's that dark feeling again. I think of the day ahead and hope the dread will pass. However, as I make my morning coffee, the image of Johnny carrying bloody canvases through Greenwich Village haunts me.

6

VJ DAY

It's VJ Day. Stands for victory over Japan back in 1945. Rhode Island is the only state in the nation that still celebrates the holiday. Banks and state offices are closed. Of course, Pearl Bones is open. We're hoping all those bankers and state workers feel the urge to spend the day in Nazareth.

Today, I read cards while Dean takes care of merchandise sales. I've put three paintings in the storefront window. Small canvases. All starry landscapes and ethereal goddesses. Perfect for the attitude of the shop. One of the paintings is bought by a young couple who is spending a few days in Nazareth. They're on their way back to Pennsylvania. The woman tells me that the colors match perfectly with her dining room. I wonder if she realizes the story I've told with that painting. I wonder if she sees beyond the bright oranges and blues and the beautiful being seated in the midst of the constellation Sagittarius.

Dean tells me he's happy with our arrangement. He hopes I'll stay longer.

"Are the crystal candle holders you ordered all stashed under the display case?"

"Yeah, pull 'em out. We might as well display the new merchandise that came in. The tourists are usually hungry on holiday weeks like this one. Those old coots bought up all I had left of the old stock last night."

I bend down, slide out a dozen or more boxes. There's a good-sized space between the bottom of the display case and the floor. "You can stick all kinds of things under here." I joke.

"Could even stash a body."

"I've thought about it many times," Dean snickers.

"What's in this box?" James Dean in *Rebel Without a Cause,* Marilyn Monroe in *Some Like It Hot,* even an old *Dracula* poster. "Hey, these movie posters are cool. We could hang some on the rack by the door." I hold one up. *"Josie and the Pussy Cats.* Here's a real classic."

"I forgot about those. I ordered them when I was on a shopping trip in New York City. Found this great shop on Broadway." He smirks at me. "Keep the *Josie* poster. My gift to you."

I'm not laughing. I often use posters of people for my artwork. I don't use real models, so images from fashion magazines and people posters work well for me. "Thanks. I may actually do a sketch from it, change it around a bit, come up with a new painting."

"You *are* the creative one, my dear."

I spread the posters on the floor. A face catches my eye; menacing gaze, a bloody knife in hand, and a black cauldron sputtering in the background. It's a poster for a movie called *Magic Man* directed by a guy named Alex Steinman, someone I've never heard of before. "Here's an odd one. Who the hell is this guy?"

"That's from a small independent film done right here. It was based on a serial killer named Cody Bartman. That's an actual photo of him."

"Creepy. Guess the movie never made it big."

"Nope, but you can find it under *Obscure Cult Classics* in video collectors' shops in New York." He looks to the door. "We've got company."

The chimes jingle. It's Gracie.

"How's it going, kiddo?" Dean surveys her dirty jeans and wrinkled shirt.

She flops in a chair near the reading table. Looks up at Dean with red-rimmed eyes. "I need a reading, Dean." She looks at me, attempts a smile.

Dean shakes his head. "Ruby will take care of you. She used

to work with me in Georgia. She's very good."

"That's cool," she says, studying the rings on my fingers. I don't know if she realizes I'm the same woman who rented her uncle's cottage.

Dean pulls me aside. "The girls got head problems—and no money, except for what she steals to buy dope. I usually try to build her confidence. Her uncle—the guy you rented that cottage from—tries, but they have their differences. She likes to come here—to talk to me. I give her *readings*. Tell her she doesn't need drugs. That she should listen to her uncle. She trusts me."

He doesn't give me a chance to tell him how much I already know about Gracie—or that I've struck up a friendship with her uncle.

"I gotta run. I have a business meeting followed by lunch over in the city. Lock up for me, will you?"

"Okay."

Dean takes a briefcase from beneath the counter, gets his keys off the hook near the register and pushes open the shop door. A black Lincoln slows down, the passenger's door swings open and Dean gets inside. I watch the car spin away. The license plate reads *JoeyG*.

"Joey Gallo could be really cute if he washed that ick out of his hair and traded in that Lincoln. Such a greaseball. I still like him though. He gets jealous when I visit Dean. Doesn't understand that he's just a friend. Too old for me." Gracie sits opposite me, watching my hands as I shuffle cards. She looks like she hasn't slept in days. Her hair is limp and dull. Her fingernails are caked with dirt. "He's really a nice guy. He bought me lunch earlier. Fries and a burger at *Bristo's*. He also told me I looked like shit and to shape up. He told me to stay away from those creeps who turn me on to dope. I only do that to irritate my uncle."

Kids.

"You know Joey good, huh?"

"I know him *real* good. He's weird. He looks all tough on the outside, but he's got a heart of gold. He says he worries about me. He's not totally banging or anything, but—"

"Banging?"

"You know, hot, hunky, but he's sort of special."

"You've got good friends then—Dean and Joey." I don't mention Michael.

"Yeah only two guys I can talk to, I guess. Joey's family's got bucks. Got a jewelry business in the city. Dean buys those unicorn charms from them.

"Dean designed this great Celtic-looking cross and it's got symbols from all religions—Islam, Pagan, about a dozen or more—etched in the metal. I helped Dean look up the symbols." She reaches inside her shirt. "My father sent me this cross. I never take it off—never. Just like I always carry my Emily Dickinson book here in my bag—all the time." The silver catches the light. "My Dad's in Seattle. I started writing to him a few months back. He says he wants to see me again one day. I haven't seen him since I was six—since my Mom took me and ran off on him. He got married again. Moved. He said to keep the cross close to my heart. That it's something that holds our souls together—like magic—like God's watching us and smiling that we're daughter and father, even though we're apart. He sent me the book too."

"All good things." I think of my own father.

She nods. Smiles to herself. Then she gazes at the bookshelves in the shop. "I like religions. They're all different, but they all keep people decent—keep them together. Dean's got books on all faiths. Anyways the cross he designed is a smash. The jewelry company is making up some for the shop." She attempts a smile. "Dean talks about stuff like that with me. He's a lonely guy. Joey's a solitary guy—but in a different way. I'm that way too. We share a lot of shit, have late-night talks a lot. He won't even kiss me until I turn eighteen. He don't know about the guys I've been with. The ones who get me high if I—" She bites her lips and taps the table thoughtfully. "I think that's why I like Joey—maybe as more than a friend. Yeah, I like him a lot despite the Lincoln and the suits." She's rambling. But her news about Joey and an innocent cross put my mind at ease about Dean's relationship with him—sort of.

"What brings you here today?"

"I feel something. It's weird. Like I'm in danger. I need to know if I should leave Nazareth. Go to my father." Her bottom lip trembles. "I mean, I'd hate to leave Joey, but—"

I continue to shuffle. "I'm picking up some strong vibes. You have family here—your uncle. He worries about you. Maybe you need to make peace with the family you have here before you visit your Dad."

"Michael doesn't understand. He wants all the wrong things for me." She pulls a bent cigarette from her blouse pocket. "Mind if I smoke?"

"Yes, I do. You shouldn't smoke."

She pouts, puts the cigarette back in her pocket.

I turn over a card. The Devil. She cringes.

I don't like the feeling the card gives me. Weird when shit like this happens—like a warning.

"It just means that you are your own worst enemy. Creating your own obstacles." I turn over another card. The Queen of Cups. "Your mother is thinking of you—" The Ten of Wands. "Maybe you could visit her."

"I miss my Mom, but Michael says I should stay away. She just fell for the wrong guy. She went with him to a package store over in Bristol. He decided to rob it. She was waiting in the car, didn't know what he was up to. He shot the clerk—in the head. My mother was charged along with him. She was just in the wrong place at the wrong time. Uncle Michael can't forgive her."

"You've got to follow your own heart. She *is* your mother." I respect Michael and think the world of what he's doing down at that house, but he doesn't understand women.

After all the years of faking it sometimes I'm amazed at the insight I have with certain people.

A vision of the old woman—Lady Lucy— flickers through my mind. Her words come back to me.

You got more talent than you think….

I turn over another card.

Death.

"Shit," Gracie says. Her eyes widen with fear.

"It's not a physical death. Just means rebirth of old ways." The Death card most definitely can mean a physical death, but it can't be true here—just can't be. Something churns in my gut. I have a feeling that this girl *could* be in danger. "Now remember what I told you about your Mom."

"Yeah, I'll think about it. Maybe you're right."

She smiles weakly, thanks me and makes her way to the sidewalk. I see her light the crooked cigarette and then disappear into a crowd of passersby.

I see the two men from the beach across the street at a jewelry stand. The red-headed man is speaking to a vendor. She's a young girl, somewhat chubby and not all that attractive. By the looks of it, the man is flirting with her. She writes something down on a pad and hands it to him—a phone number that he'll never call. The other one—the mulatto man—lifts a necklace and slides it into his pocket, then he drifts to his friend's side.

The red-headed man takes the girl's hand and kisses it.

Poor girl.

Smooth.

The men move away. A crowd forms in front of the shop window. People admire my art. It makes me smile.

The crowd clears and Lady Lucy is standing there. She's wearing a flowered dress. Smells of spices and apples seem to come from her. She holds a bouquet of dead flowers in one hand. A plastic bag from the nearby supermarket is in the other.

"I got a spell you might need."

She makes her way to the door and gives me the bag. I look inside. A plastic saint. A bottle. Shells. Some words, written on a yellowed piece of paper. Directions telling me to use holy water, bury everything in soft earth, use a strand of a lover's hair and a strand of mine. Trust in heaven and Earth.

"The last day of August. That's when the time will be right." She blinks and her eyes twinkle. "Some things will be uncovered, but there's much more beneath the surface."

She's confusing as hell, but I sense no danger from her. I feel I should listen to her, follow the directions.

A spell? Do I *really* believe in those things?

The ceiling fan swirls. A single card lifts off the top of the tarot deck as if guided by an invisible hand. The card lands face up on the floor at my feet.

The Tower.

For a moment, it looks as though there are two towers. Both

crumble before my eyes. I hear screams and blood pools around the image.

I sigh. Tears sting my eyes, then once again there's just a worn, dog-eared card at my feet.

Lady Lucy must have left when I was distracted by the card. She's not here. Not outside on the street.

Was she really here at all?

I'm still holding the shopping bag she gave me.

Clouds pass over the sun and for a moment the street darkens. Something isn't right. Last time I felt like this, Johnny Candelo got smoked.

The last day of August.

7

ANTICIPATION

The anticipation of this evening helps to get me through the rest of the day. I wonder why Dean won't be back today, why he asked me to lock up. I figure he's got a date with some woman who can't afford to let anyone know she's having a thing with him—somebody married or engaged. That's his style and that's fine 'cause I wasn't about to tell him that I'm off to a Santeria ceremony. He may think I've gone off the deep end.

In Georgia, he spent lots of his free time in the local book shops and watching movies. Other times he liked to woo the Southern ladies.

He's not a handsome man—far from it—but he has a certain *charm*. I've seen women fall head over heels for him.

I'd spend my nights painting. Most of the paintings I did back then got left behind. I wonder if those Southern ladies burned my work, thinking there was some kind of evil attached to it.

What a shame.

Those Georgian landscapes were some of my best.

Well, the past is the past. Now it's time to learn some new tricks—time to learn about Santeria—time to learn about Michael Elmira.

I've changed several times. I'm really not sure what people wear to Santeria ceremonies. A white halter dress, a dark blue blouse and skirt and several pairs of pants and shirts lay rumpled on the bed. I've finally decided that my black dress, with lace trim on the sleeves and hem, is best. I've got my boots on, knife in place. I'm wearing my usual jewelry, but I added an old pearl necklace my father gave me. He told me it was my Gramma's, but I know he stole it in Vegas. It still means a lot to me.

I make a stop at the bakery, figure I'll pick up some brownies; the least I can do when somebody has invited me to their home.

The pastries look tempting; brownies, cakes, cookies, and Danishes.

I order a dozen brownies and several Russian Tea Cakes—my favorite.

I pay the cashier and pick up two pastry boxes. The door behind me opens. A hot summer breeze floats through the store. The weatherman said rain's coming tonight.

"I see the lady has a sweet tooth."

It's Joey Gallo. He *is* quite handsome—totally *banging*—despite the slicked back hair and Mafia getup.

"Hello. It's actually not all for me."

He looks me up and down. "Didn't think so. I'm Joey Gallo. Welcome to Nazareth."

He's also very charming.

"Nice to meet you, Joey. I'm Ruby."

"I know, Dean raves about you."

"Dean and Gracie have both spoken well about you."

"They're good people." He turns to speak to the woman behind the counter. She's dressed in a pink cotton dress about five sizes too small and her tiny eyes look lost in her doughy face. "Vanessa, would you please package a dozen brownies and another half dozen of cheese Danish? I'll be back in a moment."

"Only got three cheese left, Joey." Vanessa smiles, revealing a set of badly made false teeth. I've got to get to a dentist. I'm past due for my six-month checkup. I sure as hell don't want to end up like her.

"You just want the cheese?" She smiles again. The dentures slip out of place.

Joey stifles a laugh. "It's okay. Make it three cheese and the rest blueberry…"

"You got it."

Joey turns to me. "Let me help you with this." He takes the

pastry boxes, walks with me to my van and waits until I open the door. He places the boxes on the passenger seat.

His car is parked in the next space. He's left the window down, the engine running and the radio blasting. *Putting On The Ritz,* a song that always annoyed me, is playing.

"Nostalgia. One of those songs that gets into your head and doesn't quit." I'm hoping a good dose of Stevie Nicks will cure me of that before I get to Green Briar.

"I love nostalgic music." He checks me out again. "You look very nice. I hope whomever you're meeting appreciates it."

I feel my face redden. "I'm actually off to Green Briar. Michael Elmira invited me—"

"Oh, one his ceremonies. I used to go all the time but lately, I've been researching other beliefs. I even meet some practicing witches in East Greenwich. Did you know that witchcraft is actually a healing religion?"

"I know. I knew a male witch when I lived in New York City, an Italian Strega. He was the coolest old guy." Doctor DeCaro loved to pick pockets down on Broadway, used the money to buy candles and herbs for his coven's rituals. He'd buy meals for homeless street artists too and was an advocate for them. I mourned for weeks when he died of cancer. "Witches are good people to know."

Joey smiles. "Well, have a good time tonight. I look forward to coming into the shop for one of your readings. Saw Gracie not long ago, she told me you really rock. Those were her exact words."

"She's a good kid."

"I like her a lot."

I don't know what to say. I smile. "Bye. See you again."

"For sure." His teeth are so white and straight. I wonder if his dentist is here in town.

8

SANTERIA MAGIC

I never thought I'd be spending time at Green Briar. But here I am.

I knock. I hear footsteps and then the sound of the latch turning.

I'm greeted by the blonde woman from the beach. She opens the door a crack. Allows me inside. She eagerly accepts the pastry boxes. "More food. This is great. Thanks."

She's dressed in a long white dress. Colorful butterflies and flowers are embroidered at the hem and around the scooped neck. A necklace of animal bones hangs around her neck. She notices my interest in it. "I bought it on the road," she says. "The man who sold it to me said they're fairy bones. Said he captured fairies in the woods every full moon—boiled them in soup and saved the bones for jewelry."

Michael is standing behind her. He's wearing faded jeans and a dark blue jersey, sexy even in this simple attire. "Um—Mary—shhhh." He puts his finger to his lips.

She lifts her skirt to her knees and begins to dance. She wears no shoes. Her face is peaches and cream. A lace shawl is draped around her shoulders and arms. Full lips curl into a wide smile. Her teeth are straight and white. Her hair is wild and curly; her blue eyes wide and beautiful.

"By the way. I'm Mary Dunne," she says. Her gaze falls on my silver earrings. Artist's palettes and moons and stars at the tips of paint brushes. "Are you an artist?"

"I dabble, had this great loft in SoHo once, but got a little off my course."

"I'm an artist. Want to see my work?"

"Sur—"

"I'm sure Ruby would love to see your work later, Mary," Michael says. "Right now, let her meet the others."

Mary lowers the shawl from her shoulders, exposing scars. She looks more vulnerable now. Almost afraid. I want to reach out and comfort her as I see an image of a man running a blade over her arms. Blood trickles around her. The man laughs as tears stream her face.

She shudders. Then I see canvases and the same knife slashing them, ruining acrylic landscapes and cutting painterly faces to shreds.

Michael pats Mary on the hand gently. "We'll have a little showing of your work one night—soon, okay, dear? It'll give you a chance to sort out the canvases and think about new ones you want to create. Go join the others. We'll begin in a short time."

He speaks again once we're out of Mary's hearing range. "She's had a rough time of it. Her new paintings are nothing but maddening brush strokes. No rhyme or reason to them. Can't even be considered abstract expression like Pollock did. She had exhibits in New York galleries at one time. Won a few awards. Shame. Hopefully she'll get back whatever that creep she lived with took away. She's also gained twenty pounds since she's been here. You should see her pack it away. She'll be three hundred pounds by fall if she doesn't stop."

"Sad."

"Well, she's strong despite all that. Mary has found some happiness here. She got friends and she even…um…*dates* a few men around town." He laughs, seeming to find his last comment amusing. "Gracie's got some talent too. Got a slew of drawings she did over the years, but she's letting it all go to waste now."

"She's young. I did the same when I was her age. Inspiration comes and goes. Then one day you realize what you need to do."

"I hope you're right. Now, come and meet the other residents."

Gracie sits cross-legged in a corner. She nods. Her face is

pale. She's changed her clothes and now wears a white lace dress and a wide black belt around her waist.

Michael glances her way. "You're welcome to join us, Gracie."

She shrugs her shoulders and then shifts her gaze to the floor.

"At least she's here. Most times she just goes to her room and hides out."

Michael smiles at the people waiting to meet me. "Guys, this is Ruby."

The dark-haired woman curtseys. "Ruby, this Elvira wannabee is Linda Bowes, our resident horror writer. If your reading tastes are on the dark side she is the lady to see."

"Just picked up a new Jack the Ripper book—straight from a small press in London." Linda Bowes approaches me. Black satin skirts swish. Her hair is adorned with painted barrettes—paintings of skeletons. A silver spider web is imprinted on her black shirt. Her fingernails glow with black nail polish. Sterling silver chains are draped around her neck. She wears silver sandals and her toes are painted the same black as her fingernails. Her lips are glossed with bright red. A dramatic effect with her dark hair and milky skin.

"So, you're a writer? Nice to meet you, Linda," I say.

"Nice to meet you, Ruby." She seems to purr.

I notice a tattoo of a double-edged ax on her shoulder. She turns so that I can get a better view. I touch the tattoo and gently rub my index finger over it.

"It's *Shango's* ax," says Linda. She walks away. Seems to glide. Skirts swish. Inspiration for a future painting.

I look at Michael. "*Shango'* again."

"He's quite popular." He takes my arm. "Linda has quite a collection of what she calls her research books. All you'd ever want to know about some of the most evil characters—factual and fictional—in the world."

I want to make a witty comment about axes and serial killers, but I decide it's best to bite my tongue. I'll respect Michael's beliefs and the way he uses them. At least I'll try to as long as I can. Besides—I'm here for my own research. Best not to fuck things up.

"So, Linda's a writer, huh?"

"Yeah, small press kind of stuff, but she'll make it big someday. She's talented. Now come meet the others."

The good-looking red-headed man from the beach extends his hand. He's dressed in jeans, a blue cotton shirt and sandals. "I'm Max Farino." He knows he's hot looking. "Nice to meet you, Ruby." He kisses my hand and backs away and the tall mulatto man steps forward. He's also in jeans and sandals. A colorful Hawaiian shirt hangs loosely from his shoulders. "And I am Miles Smith."

"You were all on the beach the other night."

You were also the guys who lifted the necklace from the vendor earlier.

"We were honoring summer with our dance," says Mary, her face is beaming with happiness. Somehow, she reminds me of a woman who lived in my apartment building in Boston. She'd corner me sometimes, talk about Jesus and how I could be saved. Her faced glowed the same as Mary's. Maybe that's what religion does to you—no matter what kind you have.

Another man limps into the room. He's middle-aged and short. His skin is pock-marked. His sneakers have grass stains on them and his polyester pants are about two inches too short. He's wearing a New England Patriots jacket despite the heat.

"That's Ernest," Michael says. "He's okay. Just a little slow. He lived out on the beach until I convinced him to stay here. He insisted he had to pay me back, so he brings us fresh fruit from the open-air market by the beach a few times a week. He also helps to tend with the chores—as best he can. He earns cash by working at Burger King twenty hours a week."

Ernest approaches me. Touches the laced edge of my sleeves. "Pretty."

"Ernest, this is Ruby. She's come to celebrate with us. Say hello."

"Would you like some pears or grapes, Ruby?" says Ernest as his fingers slide up my arm. I feel uneasy.

"No touching," Michael scolds.

He slumps his shoulders. "Cold in here. She sure is a nice lady."

Mary takes my hand. "Just tell him to cut it out if he bothers you. He's harmless for the most part, but—"

"But what?"

"Rumor has it he raped a woman out in Coventry."

Michael rolls his eyes and shakes his head. "Mary—that was years back—nobody ever proved—"

"I think he's creepy. I never locked my door at night until he came to live here."

"He's slow, that's all. He doesn't understand."

Mary smiles at me. "You *are* a nice lady, Ruby. I can see why *Baba* Michael digs you so much."

I feel my face flush. Michael clears his throat.

They lead me into a large hall—a ballroom from long ago. A movie plays in my head. Women dressed in long skirts and men in tuxedos twirling round and round. Mirrors line the walls and crystal chandeliers hang above. I look up at the stained ceiling where remnants of olden fixtures are rusted and broken. I close my eyes and see a man shooting a gun, another man lies in the center of the ballroom.

Ghosts. I'm sure of it. I hate when I see them.

The old black man Michael spoke to at *Bristo's* is sweeping the floor and singing quietly to himself. His clothes are ragged and faded, brown polyester pants and a Grateful Dead shirt. He looks up. His face is beaming— just like Mary's. "Hello, I'm Shelton Harold." He leans the broom against a nearby wall. He holds out his hand. "My friends call me Shelly."

I take his hand. It's warm, inviting and feels as though great love and wisdom emanate from this fragile man.

Another vision fills my head. I see Shelly dancing at what looks like the Mardi Gras in New Orleans, then sitting cross-legged in an old graveyard, where broken angels and cracked gravestones tell tales of those long dead. He's holding colored beads in one hand, a black candle in the other. The moon and planets change positions, grow dark, then bright, swell, then shrink to tiny dots of light.

He looks out the window. "The stars will be out soon. I can read them like most people read books." He looks into my eyes. I hope he doesn't see my soul. I like to keep its blemishes a secret in mixed company. "It's my pleasure to meet you, Ruby. I see special things in your eyes."

I feel relief. He doesn't know I'm a thief and a liar, or maybe he sees something beyond that. "It's really *my* pleasure, Shelly."

He nods. His eyes gleam with happiness, a wisdom which seems to penetrate my heart and soul.

Ernest paces back and forth. His gaze rests on Mary. She wrinkles her nose in disgust.

I look to the left of the ballroom. A woman weeps. She's dressed in an emerald green gown, Victorian style. She wears a silver tiara within dark auburn curls. A ruby necklace hangs around her neck. Her teardrops splatter on the polished wood floor. She watches two men carry a shrouded body away.

The scene fades. Something tells me that this room has been the scene of tragedy many times and perhaps it will be again.

Now, Michael is next to me. He's speaking softly, slowly. "This home once belonged to a prominent judge around the turn of the century. He held parties here. Everyone who was anyone attended. The historical society told me that once mirrors lined the walls and crystal chandeliers hung above," he says. "The governor was killed here—shot by his own brother. They say that two women were killed here by a drifter, twenty years before that. Some folks swear the place is haunted."

There's an altar in the middle of the room.

To the right of the altar is a cage containing three chickens. There are apples and bananas in a large bowl. Black candles burn in front of a statue of Saint Barbara. A white and red terrain is set before it. A sackcloth cape, trimmed with gold, is draped over her shoulders. Some wooden statues of Saint Joseph and Virgin Mary stare at me with large round eyes. Their robes are painted with gold leaf. They are extraordinary. A double-edged ax leans against one of the candles. A wooden cross leans against another candle. Several pairs of rosary beads are woven around it.

At Saint Barbara's feet is the silver knife Michael described to me over tea.

Max places a cross inside a bottle filled with water. "Holy water," Michael says.

Mary nudges Linda and they back into a corner and speak in hushed tones.

A familiar voice startles me. "Sorry I'm late. My battery died and I had to walk. And then I got a call—"

Dean.

Synchronism. Again.

He stops in mid-sentence. "Ruby, damn you, girl. You into *La Regla Lucumi?*"

"I'm just a guest tonight."

"Surprise," says Michael, laughing.

I laugh too. Dean joins in.

"Man, oh, man I knew you rented a cottage from Michael and all, but—"

"I figured neither one of you would admit to the other what you were up to tonight."

Dean looks at me. "Pretty silly—after all the—"

"The what?" asks Michael.

Dean is cool. "I knew Ruby when she lived in Georgia. Used to frequent the gallery where she exhibited. I've always loved her art. I'm putting some of her newer paintings in the shop window. She reads the tarot real well too. She'll be doing some readings at Pearl Bones from now on."

Neither of us mention Gracie's visit to the shop today.

"Tarot, huh?" Michael smiles. "I do divination with cowrie shells." He begins to light candles.

I tap Dean's arm. "Those shells got pictures on them?"

"Shhh, this is serious shit. Not like anything you know."

"Everybody keeps telling me it's so serious."

"Shhh. It is."

"Dean? You?"

"Yeah, me."

Dean joins Michael and the others. Mary and Linda continue to whisper to each other. Dean winks at them.

"Nice seeing you, Dean," Mary says.

"Yeah, real nice," adds Linda.

"Evening, ladies."

There's tension in their voices. Maybe the girls are just as surprised as I am to see Dean here.

He picks up a drum by the altar and begins to beat it. Shelly picks up brightly painted maracas, gives one to Ernest and they begin to shake them. Shelly is coordinated and in time with the drum's beat. Ernest gazes here and there, shakes the maraca, takes a few steps, then shakes it again.

Mary and Linda hold hands. Max and Miles stomp their feet and slap hands. Michael takes a blue and white terrain from the altar and removes some stones. Then he gently lifts one of the chickens from the cage—the knife in hand.

An altar cloth of white iridescent material shimmers in the candlelight. Skirts flutter and swirl. Hair sways back and forth with the gentle rhythms of this celebration. The drums beat louder and louder. Michael runs the blade across the chicken's neck and allows its blood to pour on the stones.

The others dance, no one is worrying if a shoulder strap slips too far down. No one cares if an old shirt is torn beneath the arm. All of them are barefoot in a maze of flowers, religious icons and glowing candles. They chant softly. Kiss each other. Despite the tattoos, the piercings, the jewelry of fairy bones and the bloody feathers, their faces take on an innocence, an ethereal quality. They touch fingers. They kiss. They go round and round, exchanging glances.

Gracie surprises me as she takes my hands. We begin to dance, moving in time with the others.

The drums. The chanting. The energy. I feel wonderful, as though I've just had a shot of whiskey or smoked a joint.

When it's over Dean asks me, "What do you think?"

"Beautiful—but the chicken."

Michael laughs at my comment, "Dinner. Mary, Linda, lets cook this offering."

Feathers float around us as he holds up the fowl.

I cringe. It's one thing to order chicken in a restaurant or to buy wings and legs in the supermarket. But this—

Michael smiles at me. "You're staying for dinner, of course."

"Are you serving potatoes with that?"

He laughs again, hard and hearty. "Actually, we can prepare some pasta and sauce for you if you choose."

"Sounds good to me," I say as Linda and Mary remove

another chicken from the cage. I don't want to wait around for it to meet its fate.

Dean leans over. "The chicken is an offering to the Orishas—the Gods. We give thanks for our blessings, life, talent, shelter, *and* for the weather heading this way—rain at last. We always eat our offerings afterwards."

"Great way to fuel the appetite," I tell him.

Dean slaps me playfully. "Hey, this isn't so bad. Legend says that the wife of *Shango'*—her name was Osa—cut off her ears and served them to him in his soup."

"Dean—" I shudder slightly.

"It's part of African myth. I'm not making it up."

Michael chuckles. "Tonight, it'll rain. You can feel it. We need it for our vegetable garden. It's been so damn hot."

"Let the others do their thing." He speaks to Dean and myself. "You guys, come have a cup of iced coffee with me on the porch."

I watch as Mary, Max, Linda and Miles make their way to the kitchen. "Chicken heads anyone?" Max chuckles.

Shelly shakes his head. "I'd better supervise. Last time Mary overcooked the chicken and Linda put too much salt in the salad. Miles and Max thought it would be funny to throw chicken heads in with the string beans. I tell you, these guys need to be watched all the time."

"I'll help. You coming along, Gracie?" Ernest holds his hand out to the girl.

Gracie wrinkles her nose. "When was the last time you showered?" She turns to Michael. "I'm going to my room. Call me when the food is ready."

"Be that way." Michael watches Gracie exit, shaking his head, hands balled into a fist. "What can you do? Anyone thirsty? Seems Shelly took care of the coffee already." Michael pours the dark liquid from a pitcher, hands me a glass.

The three of us sit cross-legged on the porch floor, share some small talk. The Ocean State Killer comes up every now and then.

"Better be careful, Ruby. You're just his type—blonde, and an artist," says Dean as he takes a strand of my hair in his fingers.

"Ruby has a spell of protection surrounding her. I sensed it the moment I met her," Michael says. He moves closer to me. "A soft blue light—an angel's light."

"Yeah, she's very special," Dean says.

The weeping woman from the ballroom drifts by. She puts her index finger to her lips. She vanishes as thunder rumbles in the distance.

Dean tilts his head, frowns a bit. Did he see her?

"Felt a chill for a second." Michael crosses his arms.

Things are getting weirder, visions, feelings, and dreams are becoming more and more potent. Is it me? Is it Nazareth? Or is it the energy of these two men? Both are magical. Both are very special.

Dean and Michael are total opposites, yet they seem to have a bond.

My bond with Dean runs deep. Partners in crime. We've never been lovers—nothing like that, but I have a special love for him.

Now Michael—there's *something* between him and me. I sense an electricity whenever he's near. I know he feels it too. This is something I haven't felt in a while. I'm tired of being alone. Maybe a short-term thing would do me good. I'm not going to fight it— I'll just let it go where it will.

You'll never have a lasting love. Never.

Dean's gaze moves from me to Michael. A knowing smile plays across his lips.

Rain is falling, splattering lightly on the pavement. Lady Lucy walks slowly past us. Her eyes are fixed on me. She's wearing a baggy black dress, with a fake red rose pinned to the collar. Bright pink sneakers adorn her feet.

Her hair is wet. The paper bag she's carrying is soaked at the bottom. "Love it when people drop stuff off in the Goodwill box. I just help myself." She lifts her dress and points a foot in my direction. "Like these? I think they're just groovy."

"Groovy?" I don't want to laugh at her. I take a gulp of my coffee.

Michael motions for her to come forward. "Very nice, Lucy. There's some chicken and vegetables for you in the kitchen.

Have one of the girls give you a plastic bag for your things too."

She climbs the stairs. Her eyes are still fastened on mine. She leans close to me. "*Shango*' watches." Her breath smells sweet, her body smells of baby powder, scented oils and something else—fresh flowers. She looks dirty and unkempt but her scent is lovely. Strange.

"Shelly has gained a lot of strength since he came here," says Dean. "A few months back he was weak and sickly. Lucky, you found him outside that old house and brought him to the emergency room."

"Yeah, I thought we'd lose the old guy before summer set in, but he's okay. Funny how some people make a comeback and others—young—just die without warning—just like that." He snaps his fingers. "He told me he cast his horoscope while he was living in that condemned house."

"What happened to him?" I ask.

"He'd been attacked by some punks. They stole his books and his religious medals. He lost a lot of blood from the knife wounds. Anyway, the stars said he'd have a setback, but his death wouldn't occur for another fifteen years or more. He swears by that stuff."

"I think about death a lot," says Dean. "Sometimes I wake up in the middle of the night and wonder if I'm going to make it through until morning."

"I know what you mean. I know what you mean," Michael says thoughtfully.

Dean nudges me. "The Religion," he says, "is something I began studying a few years back. I spent some time in Spanish Harlem, lived with somebody who was heavy into Santeria. A girl I thought I'd spend eternity with got me hooked. She was robbed and stabbed one night on her way home from work. Dead when the cops found her. We had six good months together."

I never knew Dean had real love in his life. I squeeze his hand as he continues to speak.

"When I settled here and opened Pearl Bones Michael wandered in one day looking for candles, offering bowls, odds and ends. We got talking and realized we had a lot in common. I got interested in what he was doing here. And the rest is history."

Michael nods. "You know, not too many folks in small towns take to this kind of thing. The saving grace is that we utilize the saints and many of the icons from traditional Catholic beliefs. People think I'm teaching people some kind of Charismatic Catholic New Age stuff. They see the results I get and don't ask questions. They just label me as unconventional but effective in turning these people around."

Dean shrugs, looks thoughtful. "Faith is faith, some of us just interpret it differently."

Michael raises his glass in a toast to Dean. "Bravo, my friend."

A bolt of lightning lights up the dusky sky. A chill passes over me as I watch the two men drink. I hear a woman weeping.

9

MICHAEL AND DEAN

Dinner is fun. My pasta is great.

Michael tosses a chicken bone into his plate. "I made the sauce with tomatoes from the garden. Good, Miss Ruby, or not?"

"Delicious."

I watch the men devour crispy chicken. Linda bites into a plump leg. Mary has already eaten an entire plate of chicken and potatoes. Now she's reaching for seconds. "There's apple pie for dessert," she says licking her fingers.

"You should take it easy," Michael scolds.

"Why? I don't eat that much." Mary takes a mouthful of food.

Max rolls his eyes.

"Just more to love." Mary butters a slice of bread and glares at Dean.

Dean eats heartily as well. "Don't forget the treats that Ruby brought along." Where does he put all that food?

Fresh salad, abundant with more of Michael's tomatoes, cucumbers and lettuce is served on the side. String beans and eggplant parmesan is set in large bowls.

After dessert, we drink lemonade while distant thunder rumbles.

Shelly looks tired. His movements are slow. He rubs his shoulder. "Wounds are acting up. I best be getting to bed."

"You okay?" Michael looks concerned.

"Just age and excitement doing a number on me. I'll be okay.

Got lots of life left in me. The moon is in Scorpio. I always get drained when that happens. I'll be fine once it's in a fire sign again."

"I'm going too. Want to listen to music." Ernest pushes away from the table, brushes by Mary as he leaves.

"I feel like partying." Mary takes a bite of pie and then grabs Max's hand.

Now we sit and watch Mary, Linda, Max and Miles dance. They're so light-hearted. Even Gracie is having a good time.

"Think she's starting to listen a little?" Dean asks.

Michael shrugs. "Well, to everyone but me, I guess. I think that her friendships with you and others—Joey Gallo for one—are helping." His face becomes long, solemn. He shakes his head and says softly, "She never listens to me."

"Come join us Dean," says Mary. Both she and Linda seem to scowl at him.

"Another time. I'm beat."

"The girls are frisky tonight," chuckles Michael.

"They're busting my balls." Dean pours some lemonade.

"And rightly so." Michael watches Mary stamp her feet to the music. "Glad everybody's here and it's all in fun."

That feeling of tension seems to occur each time the girls look Dean's way.

He nods his head, tries to ignore Mary as she playfully sticks her tongue out at him. "The good news is that these people aren't in jail or standing on a street corner peddling their bodies, living from trash cans—or worst."

Michael lights a cigar, passes another to Dean who cups his ear to listen to the radio blaring in the house. "Yeah, we try as best we can. Hey, radio says Providence is getting pelted with rain."

"I best be getting back before the heavy rain comes. I left the windows open. Wouldn't want your nice hardwood floors soaked," I say to my host.

Michael laughs.

Dean chugs the rest of his lemonade and then sticks his cigar in his mouth. "Give me a ride back to the shop? Got some work I need to do."

"Sure."

Dean makes his way out the screen door. I follow.

Michael takes my arm and speaks to me softly. "Can I bring a bottle of Chianti by later—about ten?"

That macho stance has returned, but I'm really starting to like it now.

"I'll make a midnight snack."

"Something exotic?"

"I bought a half gallon of Breyer's Candy Bar ice cream today. How does that sound?"

I love his laugh. "Sounds perfect."

Just go with the flow.

Max, Linda, Mary and Miles file by us and onto the front walk. They're laughing. Singing. Their voices grow faint—sound ghostly— as they disappear around the corner.

Gracie breezes by us. Makes her way into the humid night.

"Gracie, what the hell," Michael says.

"I gotta talk to Joey."

"Tell Joey he's welcome here anytime. It's been a while since he's joined us."

"He does his own thing now," Gracie shouts over her shoulder.

Dean watches her as she jogs down the street. "He'll be back. Within the past two months he's gone to a Buddhist temple in Massachusetts, attended workshops on spirits and borrowed every book in the library about Aleister Crowley—oh yeah, and we can't forget the witches."

"I did the same thing. I think you're right, he'll be back." Michael seems relieved as Joey's Lincoln pulls around the corner, slows down and takes Gracie away. "Crowley was a weird bastard."

I gaze at the pavement. It looks as though blood is trickling from a puddle and into the sewer. I blink my eyes. It's only rain.

I hear Lady Lucy's laughter ring out and blend with the thunder.

10

MELANCHOLY RAP

"Damn, Ruby, this van sounds like shit. When was the last time you had the oil changed? Had the brakes checked?" Dean runs his hand over the cracked dash.

"Was going to get rid of it when I got to Jersey. Trade it in for a small car."

"I doubt you'll get much on a trade. You really ought to think about settling—"

I change the subject. "Gracie seems like she'll be okay."

"Joey's influence more than anything. He likes her a lot, respects the fact that she's still a kid and that she's Michael Elmira's niece."

"He seems like a nice guy." I go on to tell him about our meeting at the bakery.

"He looks like a greaseball, gets a little obsessed over certain things, but he's really goodhearted." He flicks the cigar out the window. "Been painting since you've been in Nazareth?"

"I set up my easel. Remember that poster of Josie and the Pussycats?"

"Yeah? Don't even tell me?"

"I sketched the girls, made some changes. Now I'm about to do one of my vampire paintings."

"You had a whole collection of those at one time."

"Yeah, sold them to a guy who ran a place called *The Shop of the Undead* back in New York."

"Only you, Ruby."

"He happened to like my work. Lots of people make money

from ghoulish art."

"I have to admit you're damn good."

"Thanks."

"Good at some shady things too. What's your game? Is it Michael you're interested in, or were you planning on using Santeria for some new and improved scams?"

"At first, I thought I could learn some new *magics,* some things to take along with me on the road, but it seems almost sacrilegious now. And Michael, that's another story—"

"He likes you a lot. Don't go doing bad things to him."

"I won't. He's special."

"Yeah, the best."

"Did you ever see anything strange at Green Briar? Feel anything?"

"Some people have. Shelly for one." He looks at me. His eyes are twinkling. "What did you see?"

"A lady crying, dressed in green. Saw her twice."

"A Governor's wife. Went crazy after his murder. Died in the ballroom herself. Cut her wrists with one of his hunting knives."

"I hate it when I see things."

He stares ahead at the empty road.

Once again, I get the feeling that another horror will occur at Green Briar. I tap Dean playfully on the shoulder. "So, how's your love life?"

"Complicated. Can't help myself. I love women. I get into hot water all the time 'cause I can't stick to just one girl." His face is solemn. "Except for once in my life."

"Tell me about the woman in Harlem?"

"Maricia Gonzalez. She managed an herbal boutique on Fifth Avenue in Harlem."

"How'd you hook up with her?"

"I stopped at a cafeteria on Broadway for a slice of cheesecake. The place was crowded. She was sitting alone at a corner table. I asked if I could join her. One thing just led to another." His eyes are watery.

"I'm sorry you lost her. I know how it feels."

"Life goes on." He kisses me on the cheek. "Don't steal

anything on your way back home."

I pull up to Pearl Bones. "Get out before I kick you out." I'm laughing.

Dean laughs too. "See you tomorrow. I have a reading first thing in the morning. I may crash here. I do that a lot."

"Night, Dean."

"Bye."

"Dean?"

"Yeah?"

"You ever dream about Maricia? Ever *see* her?"

His face saddens. "Always. Lately it's been bizarre." He draws an imaginary circle on the window with his finger. "Something's going down. I can feel it. It happens whenever I have these dreams."

"I feel it too."

"Maybe we're just crazy people."

"I once read an article about schizophrenia. Seems my visions are symptoms of it."

Dean's not laughing, there's fear in his eyes.

I try to lighten the mood with another joke. "Get out, you lunatic."

I drive away feeling as though I've left something unfinished. Maybe I should have said something more. I look at Dean in my rearview mirror. He's standing in the rain, hands tucked in his pockets. Did he want to say more to me too?

11

A NIGHT OF WICKED SPELLS AND TENDER LOVE

I drive by *Bristo's.* Gracie is perched on the hood of Joey's car. He stands in front of her, offering her a paper plate filled with clam cakes and steamers. He's smiling. From here he reminds me of a wolf. I can't help it. Sometimes I get strange vibes about him, despite all the good things people have to say.

I figure Joey would want to keep his expensive clothes free of water marks, but the rain doesn't seem to bother either of them.

Gracie filled up at dinner, matching Mary and Dean bite for bite. If she eats anymore she'll most likely puke.

I giggle to myself as I imagine her doing just that all over Joey's fancy clothes.

I'm feeling restless. I'm still thinking about Dean. Maybe I should go back to Pearl Bones and talk to him for a while, but I wouldn't want to intrude if he's got plans to meet one of his lady friends.

A familiar unmarked detective's car passes me, slows down and then makes a U-turn. He's behind me now.

I don't feel like going home—not yet. It's not really pouring rain. The floors back at the cottage will be fine. If not, I'll skip off without paying the damages. I've done it before.

Can I really do that to Michael? Why the hell not?

I park the van near the seawall across from *Bristo's.* The detective stops a few feet behind me but doesn't leave his vehicle as I climb over the wall. I can't see his face, but I know he's watching me.

I walk on the beach. The night breeze feels good. A few teenagers are necking by some rocks. An old couple are jogging by the shore. I smell smoke and hear soft chanting.

From behind a dune I see Mary and Linda sitting cross-legged on the sand. A small fire burns in front of them.

Mary holds a cloth doll in her hands. She puts a match to its chest.

"Bastard two-timed us."

"Yeah, burn in hell, Dean." Linda snatches the burning doll from Mary and watches the flames eat away at it.

A gaping black hole appears in the doll's chest. Mary flings the Dean image into the flames.

"Two-timer," they say in unison.

Mary brushes the sand off her clothes. "Let's go to the ice-cream shop for a sundae after we do our ritual stabbing." She takes another doll out of her pocket.

Linda gazes at the fire. "Not me. I won't eat for days now. That meal was too much. I'll meet you back at the house later, but let's do our *hit* here first." She pulls a large hat pin out of her purse.

Both women burst into laughter.

I sneak away quietly. I hadn't realized there was a love triangle brewing back at the house, an explanation for the tension I sensed. I know the spell is just a way of relieving their anger. Dean's got to learn to cool it with women. He's going to get himself into something he can't fix one day. I hope I'm not around to see it.

Funny how his true love died violently—just like Johnny. I hope we've both seen enough events like that in our lives.

I wonder again if he wanted to say more to me.

Hot. So hot. Despite the rain it's like an oven in here. Every now and then a breeze slips through the window above my bed. Just a tease. The heat wave has affected the entire country. No relief in sight. Ninety-five degrees today. One hundred degrees tomorrow.

It's midnight. Michael hasn't shown. I'm too damn tired. I slide between cool sheets.

I'm groggy with sleep. Don't know if I'm dreaming as I hear breaks screech. People are yelling. Gracie's voice? I'm too weary to prop myself up and peer out the window. Is Michael saying something?

I drift to sleep, think I hear somebody crying as I dream. Is it the lady in green? Gracie? Most likely my imagination getting the best of me again. I'm falling— earth—freshly turned—a cross, just like Gracie's. Somebody's reciting poetry. Sounds like Dickinson. The New York skyline looks different. Something's missing.

Johnny. He's sitting in a doorway in lower Manhattan. There's soot and ashes on his clothes. The lady in green is sitting by his side, playing cards are spread out on the pavement. He looks at me, dark circles beneath his eyes and a bullet hole in his head. *We know all the secrets. Listen as hard as you can.*

I still love you, Ruby girl.

I miss that son-of-a-bitch.

It gets lonely, this hustler's life, though the impact of loneliness doesn't slap me in the face too often. Only when I see a young couple glance at each other over their baby's stroller at the grocery store, or when a soft rain taps like a magic drum at my window—when I'm lying in bed alone. Rare moments. Most times I hang tough, don't let reality sink in as deep as it ought to.

It's two in the morning. The rain is coming down hard now. Lightning brightens the pitch-black bedroom. What did the fortune teller say?

Shango'

And what did Dean say?

Sometimes I wake up in the middle of the night and wonder if I'm going to make it through until morning.

I'm frightened all of a sudden. I never worried about dying before—but I'm scared now.

I don't want to be alone tonight.

Did I put my knife under my pillow, or did I leave it inside my boot?

I hear a gentle knock on the windowpane above my bed. Michael. Thank goodness. His hair is wet, clinging to his skin. I tell him to go around to the kitchen door.

"Sorry I didn't get here earlier. The basement gets flooded when it rains hard. Shelly and I had to get the pump running before I could leave." His eyes look sad. "Poor old guy. I had to wake him."

He has flowers. A bottle of wine. There's something wrapped in tissue paper.

I take his gifts, unwrap the tissue. It's a maraca, painted red and white.

"It's heavy—but quite beautiful."

"There's stones and sand inside it."

"I love it."

He says, "Just shake it when you're in danger. They say that *Shango*' will come to help you."

I don't say anything. I just stand on my tiptoes and kiss him.

He touches my face. There's some dirt on his hands. "It's wet and sloppy out there. Mud splattered everywhere."

I laugh. "Go wash your hands."

I put the maraca on top of the refrigerator. The flowers go in a vase. Matty scurries under the bed.

We sit on the couch. We drink our wine. Eat dishes of ice cream.

He takes my hand, chuckles as Matty enters the room, looks at him and growls.

"He gets jealous," I say. His hands are warm.

"It's been a while—this kind of thing."

"For me too."

"You must have boyfriends everywhere."

"Yeah right." I feel my face flush.

"I was married. Lasted nearly ten years and then she got bored with me—especially with my teacher's salary. She didn't understand what I was trying to do at Green Briar. She wanted to remodel it, turn it into one of those houses you see in *Good Housekeeping*."

"People drift apart. Doesn't mean one is right and the other is wrong. They just want different things in life."

"Right now, I want a girl named Ruby."

My heart skips a beat, my free hand goes limp and ends up

in a bowl of melted ice cream.

Did I mention that I can be a real klutz at times?

He doesn't laugh at me. He just licks my fingers, then he kisses me hard. Pretty soon he's caressing my breasts and his hands move slowly up my night shirt. He lifts it carefully, removes my panties and slides his fingers in and out of me. He spreads my thighs and gently enters me. Lightning and thunder dance—play a serenade as he loves me. I feel his semen explode inside me. There's something new inside me as well—creation—life. I swear I can feel it.

Later in bed he takes me again. This time it's slower, more understood. Our bodies meet like they were made for each other.

This isn't just fucking, it's something real, something special that I'll always keep with me—no matter what happens.

12

THE DARKNESS BEGINS

The gas gauge on my van is near empty. "You shouldn't let it go past half a tank. Bad for the gas line," Michael scolds. "Let me drive you to the shop. I'll take a look at the brakes and change the oil for you. I'll pick you up later."

"Fill it with gas?"

"The woman is already wrapping me around her little finger."

On our way to Pearl Bones we see Max and Miles sitting on a bench near a bus stop. They wave at us. Max's jacket is zipped up to the top. It looks like he's hiding something underneath.

Michael says, "Looked like they were up to something."

"You never know," I say, guilt filling me as I think of my own crimes

"Those two have a history of breaking and entering."

"If anybody's been robbed or worse, I'm sure we'll find out soon. This is a small town. News travels fast in places like this," I tell him.

"No doubt."

Something is wrong.

"I'll check back here about noon. I'll get some pizza from the restaurant on the corner, okay?"

"Okay."

"Looks like you've got company already." A woman is standing by the shop door.

"The horse lady," he murmurs.

"The who?"

"Likes to bet the horses. Rumor has it she's married to a bookie. Even owned a couple of racehorses years back. Lots of scandal with the gaming commission. If you see any sure things in her reading call me."

I slap him playfully. "I'm not that talented."

"I happen to think you're very talented." He touches my hand and a feeling of sadness fills me.

"Hmm, thought Dean would be here. That the shop would be open. He said he might sleep here. He must have gone home after all—maybe called a cab". I shrug my shoulders.

"Never know with him. He could have called *somebody* to fetch him. He's been courting a woman in the next town—and a few others."

"He's quite the womanizer. Pisses a lot of chicks off."

"No shit, Mary and Linda got wise to him. Said they were getting even."

"I spotted them on the beach last night. They had voodoo dolls—"

Michael laughs out loud. "Two crazy wenches." He leans over to kiss me. "See you later."

"Sure will," I answer as I climb out of the truck.

The woman outside the shop smiles at me. "No sign of Dean. He said he'd be here for my reading promptly at nine."

"I'll take care of it."

With the woman close behind me, I nudge the door open with my shoulder. It opens.

Something *is* wrong.

I turn on the lights and spread the embroidered cloth on the card reading table.

"I'll look around," says the woman. "I wanted to take a peek at the new candles he put out."

"Take your time."

I need a deck of cards. I check the box Dean keeps by the table. *The Chiromancian of Mrs. Indra*—the cards are too big and hard to shuffle. Great artwork though. I toss the deck back in the box. *Tarot Balbi*—the pictures are boring. *Ecletic Tarot*—the damn things are in Austrian. *The Robin Wood Tarot Deck, The Celtic Tarot, The Tarot of Love.* Does Dean really use all of these decks? They're worn, have a distinct used look. He's a hot shit, that one. "Ahh, this is what I want." *The Rider Tarot Deck*. It's what I like to use. It's what I keep in my own stash of goodies. What I'm most familiar with. I suppose I could fake it with another. I've had to before. But why work harder than I need to?

Where the hell is Dean?

I check his appointment book by the register. He's scribbled down the woman's name. Mrs. Katherine Baldwin. A small woman who looks to be around sixty- five. Her hair is dyed flaming red and she's wearing a lime green short set.

I look outside to see if there's any sign of Dean. Max and Miles walk by. They're both drinking *Dunkin' Donuts* coffee. They wave.

I sigh. Still looked like there was something stuffed beneath that jacket. No matter, let's take care of this lady for now.

"Ready now, Mrs. Baldwin?"

She sits, smooths down her blouse, bats her caked eyelashes and says, "Tell me about my health?"

I hate when they ask that. Why don't they just go to a doctor? Do I look like a family physician?

I smile. "Oh, you're quite healthy. You'll live to be one hundred."

She smiles. Her false teeth are yellow with smoke stains.

"I'm going down to Foxwoods casino this weekend. Gonna play some slots. Maybe bet on a televised horse race. Got any numbers for me? Horses names?"

An image flashes through my head.

"All I see is a gray horse. The jockey is wearing red."

"Sammy's Gal is gray. Was thinking of betting on that philly, but a jockey named Slinky Demosa is riding her. He ain't done a thing since last winter and I don't play girl jockeys—never do. You know why?"

I shake my head.

"They ain't got the strength in their arms like the guys do. Oh sure, they win sometimes—but I say it's fixed. The guys give them the race if they give head. I play a race by studying how many times they won. If they like the mud. Shit like that. I don't ever play long shots. You only throw your money away." She makes stabbing motions at the cards with her index finger. "Lots of racing scams through the years. My husband knew a commissioner. If you paid the guy a hundred bucks he let the horse owners get away with anything—like horse switching."

"Horse switching?" I remember my dad using the term.

"Ya know, when the horses look alike, but you replace the slow horse with a fast one. Ohhh, I know the horse racing business like the back of my hand."

She bites her lips nervously. "You don't see any underhanded stuff—um, I mean on my end?" she asks.

I look at the cards and see the old woman with a cigarette hanging from her lips. She's counting money.

"Nothing like that." Nothing specific anyway.

The next half hour is filled with queries and concerns about mundane daily matters.

The timer rings. Mrs. Baldwin flinches.

"Dean was preparing a love sachet for me. Said it'd be ready today. I married a guy seventeen years younger than me. Lately—he's um…been having problems. Thinks it matters to me. I'm sixty—well, sixty-five in October. What do I care about a roll in the hay? But I gotta humor my husband, make him think I still want him. Dean thought a nice sachet under his pillow at night might help."

"Gee, Mrs. Baldwin, Dean isn't here. I haven't a clue where he'd put your sachet."

"Look behind the counter, dear. Under the sterling silver pentagram shelf." For a split second, she reminds me of Mrs. Hudson, the way she just tilted her head, the way she called me *dear.* I wonder how the old broad is.

"Okay," I smile, rise from my chair and go behind the counter.

The sachet is right where Mrs. Baldwin said it would be.

But there's a pool of blood in between the witch's pentagram and a dragon's eye.

A hand slides out from the space between the bottom of the display case and the floor. A foot. Strands of long hair.

Dean.

His eyes are filled with terror. Blood is gushing from his chest.

"Shhh."

I stand up quickly. The woman is before the register. Best not to let on to this woman that Dean's lying there with a knife wound in his chest. Best to just get her out of the way and then call for help.

Mrs. Baldwin opens her purse. "How much?"

"Thirty bucks."

"What about the sachet?"

"It's on the house."

"Oh, thank you. Thank you. Such a good reading, too."

"Goodbye Mrs. Baldwin."

She isn't stupid. She's looking right into my eyes. She sees my panic, senses my fear. "Something's wrong." She takes my hand. "Is that blood on your fingers?"

I hadn't noticed myself.

Before I can stop her, she's made her way around the counter.

"Dear Lord in Heaven. Call 911. Let's not touch anything under here. We'll mess up the police evidence. I watch a lot of those crime shows."

"Mrs. Baldwin, please—"

"Just make the call. He's still alive." She pulls a pair of rosary beads out of her purse. She perches herself on the counter and she begins to pray.

I call 911, then I kneel beside Dean. "What the hell happened?"

"Gracie—she—"

"I didn't see anybody except those two guys from Green Briar—Max and Matt—or whatever their names are. They were sitting on the curb," Mrs. Baldwin says in between a Hail Mary. "That Max character was holding up his shirt, jiving about some girl he'd met at an all-night club. Girl wrote her number and a note on his belly in magic marker. Said he had to pull down his pants to see the rest of what she wrote."

Dean shakes his head and tries to speak again. "Don't talk. Don't move until the paramedics get here," I tell him.

Mrs. Baldwin tells me she'll lock up the shop and the

register. She gives me her number and asks me to call her later. I thank her and impulsively kiss her on the cheek. I see a younger Mrs. Baldwin. She's holding two photos up to an overhead light. Photos of horses. The animals look like twins, maybe it's even the same horse, but I know better. *Horse switching*—isn't that what she called it? Hey, we've all got our faults. All got our scams. She's a good person inside.

Blood trickles from the corner of Dean's mouth. He wheezes and his eyelids flutter. I touch his face and brush a strand of hair from his forehead. I hope for the best, but know deep down that things will turn out bad.

13

DETECTIVE MANSI

I ride with Dean to the hospital. He's lost a lot of blood.

They check him into a room. Say he's not out of the woods. I'm allowed to stay with him. He tries to talk. He holds my hand. His skin is so cold.

A detective arrives. He looks to be about forty. He's wearing a gray sports jacket with a Boston Red Sox shirt underneath. He's got on black jeans and a pair of designer sneakers. He's nice-looking in a tough sort of way. His hair is dark, just like his eyes. Looks like he didn't bother to shave this morning. It looks good on him. He has an arrogant air. Looks at me like I'm under suspicion.

I *know* he's the same guy who followed me last night. The same guy who was cruising by the beach when I arrived in Nazareth.

He's talking softly on a cell phone, every now and then his eyes dart to me. He doesn't smile, doesn't seem all that friendly.

Dean tugs at my fingers. "Careful." He looks at the detective.

Elated that Dean can say more than just Gracie's name, I lean close to him and ask, "Who did this to you, Dean? Who?"

He closes his eyes, drifts away from me.

The cop ends his conversation, clips the phone to his belt then pulls a small pad from his breast pocket. Looks me straight in the eye. "I'm Detective Mansi. What's your full name?"

"Ruby Nicholas."

"Can you tell me what happened?"

I tell him about how I found Dean. He listens and writes.

"Who's Gracie?" the detective asks.

"Michael Elmira's niece. Comes into Dean's shop— Pearl Bones. Knows him pretty well."

"Oh, yeah. He's brought her to the station on more than one occasion." He shakes his head. "What's your relationship with the victim?"

"Friend from way back. He recently hired me to work in his shop."

"You're new in town. Where'd you blow in from?"

Be careful. My heart flutters a bit. "Denver, Colorado. Spent some time in New York City. I'm an artist and—"

"Oh, yeah? You any good?"

"Some people think so."

"Lots of artists in Nazareth. They crowd the walks, piss off the merchants. None of them are much good. If they were they'd be in galleries, museums, no?"

"It's tough to get a break."

He smirks. "Artist types are trouble, radical, unable to hold down real jobs most times."

"That's not always—"

"Thank you, Ms. Nicholas. I'll phone Michael Elmira. We'll talk to the girl."

"By the way, Detective—"

"Yes?"

"You might want to talk to Max Farino and Miles Smith. They've been hanging around and—"

"Petty thieves, but I'll talk to them."

"Thanks."

The detective looks me up and down. "Denver, you said?"

"Yeah." Is my face turning red?

"Miss, you're not a suspect, but I suggest you stay in town until this matter is settled."

Where have I heard that before?

14

SHELLY'S CONFESSION

Tonight, there is a small ceremony at Green Briar. Max, Mary, Linda, Miles, and Shelly have joined Michael and me in the ballroom.

"Ernest won't come out of his room," Shelly says as he lights a candle. "Keeps saying that too many bad things are happening."

There are white candles burning in the windows. A beautiful bronze crucifix hangs above the altar. "Got it when I was in Boston last winter." Max smiles proudly.

"Not from that Christian bookstore where the hot brunette worked? How did you convince her to give it you? It's a little too big to slide into your pocket." Miles shakes his head.

"Do you think I *steal* everything?"

No one answers. It would have been comical under different circumstances.

Michael looks up at the crucifix, then at Max, then moves close to my side. "Let's form a circle." We all hold hands and wait for him to invoke *Shango*'.

He's placed some bananas, a red ribbon and a bowl painted with red trim on the altar.

"Protect our brother Dean from harm and death. Accept our offering." He sighs. "Please bring Gracie back to us. Let her be safe."

He covers one banana with a piece of gold cloth and ties it with a red ribbon. He repeats this with three more bananas—four times in all. Every time he ties the red ribbon he asks

Shango' to watch over Dean—to grant Gracie's safe return.

He places the bananas in the bowl then lights a red candle.

"It's done for now. When the bananas rot you're supposed to bury them under a Palm tree. This is New England. An old apple tree will do."

"Does it work?" I ask.

"Do novenas, rosaries or high masses work? Perhaps in the end it's all up to the gods—or God."

Shelly removes the red candle from the altar, places it on the floor and sits across from it. "When I lived in Louisiana we had some nice traditions. Whenever something bad went down, whenever somebody close was sick, or in danger, we'd have *The Telling Time*. Just talking, *telling*, each other about the ones we've loved and lost. It works best with deceased lovers, parents and siblings. They tend to stay close to us after death. They say the *telling* feeds them. The healing seeps into the candle's flame as we speak. Spirits rise up and go to the one who needs the healing." He looks at the candle's flame. "It's a good thing to do right after a ceremony. There's magic in the air from the invocation. The veil between life and death is thinner."

Michael sits to Shelly's right. I sit to his left.

Michael says, "Sounds like what witches do on Halloween. Sit around and tell stories about their families, the dead in particular. Makes it easier for the living and the dead to touch each other."

The others sit on the floor, one by one. Everyone is quiet, just staring at Shelly.

Michael watches as a thin spiral of smoke rises from the candle. "Shelly, you start. I don't know if everybody here will open up, but whomever wants to speak after he's finished, feel free."

Shelly sighs. "Okay, you bunch of chicken livers, I'll say what I got to say and then maybe Michael or Ruby can go next."

I cringe. I can't talk about Johnny. No way. There's my dead uncle, but he wasn't exactly one of God's saints either.

The lady in green hovers by a window.

A car speeds by, black, shiny, Joey's Lincoln.

Johnny talked about buying a Lincoln. Best not to think

about him now, even better not to mention him.

Shelly looks at me. "It's okay, Ruby, we all got secrets. Listening is good too."

Was he reading my mind?

He chuckles, then begins to speak. "I used to be a pretty good piano player in my younger days. Now my hands are filled with arthritis, not much good for anything except holding a broom or lifting a fork. I was a pretty handsome guy too. Had a full head of hair. Women told me I had great eyes.

"New Orleans was a hotbed for musicians and for singers like Maya Colby. Maya was a white woman. These days it's no big thing for a black man and white woman to fall in love, but back in the 50s, especially down South, it wasn't considered right. To make things more complicated Maya was a married woman. Her husband was into shady things; dope, illegal gambling, and prostitution just to name a few.

"The first time Maya walked on the stage and sang I felt that feeling. You know the one. She was blonde. Her eyes were smoky blue. She was curvy like a movie star."

I close my eyes and see a handsome man dressed in a gray silk suit, a rose in his lapel. A beautiful blonde woman, decked out in a blue-sequined gown and dripping in diamonds, leans seductively against his piano.

Shelly whispers in my ear. "You see it don't you, Ruby?"

"Yeah."

He takes my hand. "I didn't realize she felt the same until the night she asked if she could buy me a drink. I accepted. We did more talking than drinking. Wasn't long until we were meeting in hotel rooms off the highway."

I see lovers tangled on white sheets. I see a black car, like a phantom, parked outside their window.

"One night Mitchell Colby and his brutes busted into our room, two of them dragged me out and beat the shit out of me. Mitchell and one other man stayed inside with Maya. They busted one of my arms, split my lips and broke a few ribs."

I know they did something awful to Maya.

Shelly squeezes my hand. "They took me to the state border. Mitchell handed me a burlap bag. I remember his exact words,

'Black boy, what you long for is inside, 'cause you still want Maya bad, don't you?' He laughed. Spittle dripped down his chin. 'You're cursed because of the color of your skin, always will be. I figure by leaving you alive you'll have hard luck all your life. Maya, on the other hand, was lily white, until you fucked her. You damaged her. No white man, including myself, will want to touch her again.' He spit on the ground then moved real close to me. I thought he was gonna hit me again, but he just kept on talking. 'Don't open that bag until we're out of sight. Don't set foot in New Orleans again.'

"I watched the car disappear down the highway. Was scared out of my wits. I must have waited for hours.

"Then I opened the bag. Inside was one of Maya's smoky blue eyes, and half of her left hand. I buried the bag in a cornfield and hitched all the way to Providence."

Nobody speaks. I hug Shelly. Tears drip down his face. "It was a long time ago."

The candle's smoke billows. It curls and rises to the ceiling.

"Sorry, Shelly, that was a shitty thing to have gone down," says Max.

"I think we've all got things to talk about, but I'm not ready right now," Miles adds.

"All in good time. The *telling* has helped me release some of my own pain." Shelly gives my hand another squeeze.

The candle's smoke is thicker, spiraling round and round. The flame is swaying back and forth. The lady in green is gone.

"I think Maya's spirit will find its way to Dean. Bring him some healing, or at least some comfort. Maybe it can guide our Gracie home."

"Anyone else care to talk?" Michael asks. "Not tonight," says Max.

Michael pats Shelly on the back. "Thank you."

Tonight, I dream of Dean. He's lying in his hospital bed and Maya is sitting on its edge. She's singing an old blues song from New Orleans. It's so sad. Dean is crying bloody tears.

I have no other dreams—just deep sleep.

15

DEALING THE HIGH PRIESTESS

Mary is minding Pearl Bones. I promised her a reading in return.

I'd wanted to plant the herbs I'd bought at the country store this morning, but I spent the time with Dean. There's no change. He's still not talking. They tell me it's because of the trauma.

I do a tarot reading after I leave Dean. The High Priestess is the first card I turn over. When a fortune teller deals that card it normally implies that there are secrets— mysteries which must be uncovered.

I remember the dream I had of Johnny and the lady in green. He said they knew *all* the secrets.

The priestess is sitting, dressed in layers of blue veils.

She holds a book, but you can't read what's inside.

A wise mystic will tell you that she's asking you to look inside yourself, beneath the layers of mystery—the answers are there.

Dealing the High Priestess is like trying to interpret an ancient riddle—you'll have access to sacred rites if you look into the face of God—or the Devil himself.

Maybe that's what I have to do to solve the riddle of Nazareth—of Dean's attacker—of Michael.

It's noon. The shop is empty, except for Mary. She's reading a book on Moon phases. "Just curious. I like to check out planetary alignments when significant things happen. I'm trying to see what sign the moon was in at the time of Dean's attack. Looks like Scorpio."

"Scorpio rules knives and an assortment of unsavory things." I try to remember Mrs. Hudson's Astrology lessons. She studied for a while by mail order. Had tons of books on the subject. "It's mysterious, sexual and intense."

Mrs. Hudson and Shelly would probably get along. Mary turns a page. "Says here that it's ruling sign is Pluto. Pluto is the Lord of Death."

"Dean's not going to die." The doctor said he was in stable condition, but that could change either way.

Mary shrugs her shoulders. "Dean's tough. I'm not really worrying about him."

"Want that reading now?"

"Sure."

"I'm really not that good."

"Then you won't see how evil I really am."

I pick up the *Rider Waite* deck.

"Shuffle. Think of a question you want answered."

She shuffles. Hands the deck back to me.

I take three cards from the top, turn them face up.

The Ten of Swords, The High Priestess and Death. "Don't look too promising."

"I know what it means."

"Yeah?"

"The Swords are Dean's pain and suffering. The High Priestess means things are hidden. And Death could mean that you're thinking the worst." I give her a smug look. "You're trying to solve the mystery of Dean's slayer and fearing the worst."

Her face flushes. "No, my question was about *me*. I'm still angry at Dean for the way he two-timed Linda and me. See, I *am* evil. I mean, I *do* feel bad, nobody should have to go through that."

"It wasn't right what he did. I can understand, but what *did* you ask the cards?"

"I wanted to know if I'd have a bright future."

"Somebody told me once that the cards often ignore your conscious questions and—"

She touches each card with her index finger. "Looks like somebody is going to stab me. He lives a secret life and my wounds will be fatal." Her face is serious.

"The cards are bunk." The feeling of dread overtakes me.

"I've always been afraid that Bennie would come after me."

"Who?"

"My ex."

"He hurt you?"

"Beat the crap out of me, cut me, ruined my work."

"Want some tea? I'll boil some water."

We sit with tea cups before us. The cards are tucked in their cardboard box.

"I've been having bad dreams. Been having this bad feeling too. I always had the dreams and the feelings before Bennie went on one of his drinking sprees and hit me."

What the hell. What's this rash of dreams and feelings lately?

"How long were you with Bennie?"

"A couple years. I met him when I was a junior at Parsons. Bennie was a senior."

"Parsons in New York City?"

"Yeah, a long time ago. He's a painter too. He'd even had a few shows before he graduated. He knows a lot of people in the art world, good connections who make things happen for him."

"But is he good?"

"He's an abstract expressionist. As far as I'm concerned, he mimics Pollock and a lot of the early pioneers of the movement, but like they say, *it's who you know.*

"I met him at one of his shows. I was thinner then. He noticed me looking at one of his pieces, a huge canvas with purple and yellow splatters over a deep red background." Her eyes light up with amusement. "I didn't really like it. I wasn't that impressed with any of his work, but he'd gotten some good reviews and people were talking about him. I'd seen his picture in the newspaper and thought he was good-looking, so I went to his opening, dressed in a slinky black dress. Had my hair done and spent one hundred and fifty bucks on a necklace in a designer jewelry shop."

"Did he ask you out that night?"

"Yeah, I slept with him that night. We went to my apartment

in Brooklyn and he never left. He was being evicted from a townhouse in Manhattan. Told me he knew he couldn't afford to stay there, but wanted to live there, even if it was just for a while. Said the view was spectacular."

"Such a rebel. Sounds romantic."

"The romance was gone quickly. He was on a giant ego trip, drank a lot when the reviews weren't kind. He had some work hanging in a snooty gallery in SoHo. They had drawings by Picasso and John Lennon hanging side by side in a room filled with black leather chairs and glass tables. A Chagall hung over the reception desk. This was really big time for Bennie. They'd chosen two of his landscapes to hang in a group show. The critics loved everyone but Bennie. They said his work was immature. He drank heavily after that."

"That happens. You've got to roll with the punches."

"I was the one who *took* all the punches. When a small gallery in Chelsea sold one of my paintings and asked if I'd be interested in a solo show—" She starts to cry.

"What happened?"

"He slashed all the canvases, slashed me a bit too. Then he beat the crap out of me, broke two of my fingers and dislocated my shoulder. It still snaps out of place when it's damp, or when I'm tired."

"Shit."

"I'd been to Nazareth on vacation with my parents when I was a kid. Always loved it here. I hopped a train, came here and still live in fear that he'll find me."

"Tell me about your dreams, if you want."

"I'm painting in the ballroom, really getting back to being the artist I used to be. There's somebody else there, a woman. She's in green. She screams when Bennie bursts in and goes crazy on me, cutting my arms and shoulders with a knife, snipping strands of my hair and the tips of my nails with scissors. I don't know if I live or die. I always wake up before he sticks the knife in my chest. Last thing I see is that woman. She's wiping blood off the floor."

I have dinner with Michael tonight. He brought over fresh

vegetables from his garden; eggplant and tomatoes. I made eggplant parmesan.

I'm wearing a baggy old shirt and a pair of pants with a drawstring waist. I feel shitty and fat tonight.

Michael looks sexy in tight jeans and a tight black shirt.

"You feeling okay? You look pale, like something's wrong."

"I'm fine. Just stressed." I'm not sure that it's entirely stress.

"No sign of Gracie," Michael says as he sips red wine. "She told Miles she wanted to head South."

"Too bad. I hope the kid straightens out."

"Doubtful. Very doubtful. Detective Mansi came around Green Briar today and asked some questions about her. He told me Dean said her name a few times before he blacked out."

"He did, but he was delirious according to the doctors. Probably doesn't mean a thing."

"I hope they're right. I'd hate to think she had anything to do with what's been happening."

"Me too." That sense of forboding comes back to torment me.

Our lovemaking grows more intense each time we're together. Tonight, Michael hurts me as he pins my arms down. His hands move over my breasts and shoulders roughly. His body pummels against mine.

Johnny did stuff like that too. Even used handcuffs on a few occasions. Tied me up. He knew what he was doing. I trusted him.

I see Johnny's face in front of me—not Michael's as he wraps his fingers around my neck. I can't breathe. Tears stream down my face.

When I cry out he tells me he's sorry. Then Michael becomes the gentle lover I know.

Tonight, I fall asleep thinking of how that feral and cold look remained in his eyes—even after his apology.

My hand dangles off the side of the bed. Matty licks my fingers. He won't sleep beside me when Michael is here.

Most times he growls at Michael when they're in the same room together. I wonder if it's jealously, or that sixth sense that cats possess.

Matty was a gift from a wealthy and eccentric sculptor, named Lily Brent. She befriended Johnny and me when we met at a gallery opening in Tribeca. She told us she knew us from another lifetime, most likely from ancient Jerusalem.

She lived in the Upper East Side, had this amazing house, which was once a funeral parlor. When the owner passed on, the place was put up for sale. Lily's dark obsession with all things dead quickly prompted her to purchase the building. She'd have séances there at least once a month.

Johnny and I attended her *gatherings* on several occasions. Once the ghost of the departed funeral home owner appeared, scolding Lily for making too many changes on his property.

There was always a dozen or more people at these things. Only she and Johnny and I ever saw the ghosts.

When her pet feline, Magdeline, gave birth to a litter of five kittens, she presented us with the only male in the group, said she had a vision. John Lennon told her the little guy was meant to be with us.

Matty loved Johnny. Never growled at him. Loved to sit on his lap. He cuddled in between us when we slept.

Sleep.

Johnny's here. He takes my hand—like always.

Crows circle above church spires. The streets are crowded—but not with the living. Ghosts say good evening to us, some gather on tops of buildings, look down at us with soulful eyes, and point to the road beyond.

We come to a house by the water.

"Who lives here?" I ask

The man who holds the Seven of Swords.

We walk down stairs. There's a bolted door, but in dreams it doesn't matter because dreams break all the rules. And we walk through the door.

A little girl sits cross-legged on the floor. It's dark, and there are drawings pinned to damp walls. She holds a vellum pad on her lap, clutches her pen and makes cross- hatching lines.

A candle flickers. Its flame grows larger as the girl continues to work.

She holds up her masterpiece. It's Gracie's face.

We're in love. We need the blood.

Was that Gracie's voice?

The girl disappears as the drawing tumbles and flips through the air.

Now she's standing in the corner, blonde hair wet from the rain, jeans ripped at the knees. Just like a photo my dad carries around—a photo of me at five.

I wake to the sound of Matty tapping on the window, tiny cat calls in the night.

I hear Lady Lucy outside. She's singing. It's something soft and somber.

The dreams will be even more powerful soon.

Does the woman ever sleep?

I peek out the window. See her skirts billowing in the mid-August wind. She's carrying a basket. Every now and then she reaches inside, gathers rose petals and sprinkles them on the pavement.

She walks into a smoky cloud of fog and disappears. I no longer hear her as the flower petals are swooped up by a breeze.

Was that blood dripping from her hands?

16

MURDER AT GREEN BRIAR

Dean died two nights ago. We buried him this afternoon.

"Back to Mother Earth, old friend," Max said as his voice cracked.

Miles stood there, hands shaking, eyes lowered.

Michael put coins over each of Dean's eyes. "For the ferryman. Don't want him coming back and picking my pockets for his fair to the other side."

Linda put a solitary rose on his chest.

"The moon will shine just above his grave," said Shelly.

"I'll miss you like hell," I whispered, kissing him goodbye.

Joey arrived late, put one of the crosses he and Dean had worked on inside the casket. He mumbled something incoherent as the silver reflected in the sun. He smiled sadly, "You've got more than enough to get across the river now, old boy."

Mary didn't show up. I can't believe that she refuses to forgive Dean—even now.

Gracie is still missing. Detective Mansi says he's keeping an eye out for her.

I'm so tired these days. Haven't had a period in a while. I know I'm carrying Michael's baby. I'm not sure if I want him to know.

The heat wave has passed and sometimes the nights are cool and damp.

The apples on the tree next to my cottage are green. In a few weeks, they'll be sweet and ready for picking.

I guess *Peal Bones* is mine—my responsibility until I can

make further arrangements.

I never intended to settle in Nazareth. "Why'd you have to leave that will, Dean? Why'd you have to complicate everything by dying?" I wipe tears from my eyes.

I really have to go soon. It's going to be hard, but I have to.

I'll put the shop up for sale. Leave it in Michael's hands if he's not too miffed at me for splitting.

Time to do Lady Lucy's spell. What the hell. What harm can it do? Imagine. Me, of all people, actually thinking a spell can work.

Faith.

That's what Michael calls it. That's what it all boils down to.

Mrs. Baldwin took care of the shop for me today. She's been helping out a lot.

"That boy always did me good, Ruby. Anything I can do. Anything," she says.

"Free readings and eight bucks an hour, that's all I can offer," I answer.

"I don't need the money, love. Just give me the readings. Don't worry about a thing."

I checked with her after the burial. Then I went by the cottage to make sure Matty had enough food. We all agree to meet back at the house at five. It's almost five thirty now. I wonder why there's police cars outside. Then I realize there's a coroner's car here too.

I make my way inside. Michael is standing in the hall talking to Detective Mansi, who eyes me suspiciously as I approach.

"Well, Ruby, seems you usually appear after one of these fatalities as of late."

"Excuse me—"

The lady in green hovers over the doorway. She's weeping. I hear nothing, not others talking, not policemen working, not the traffic outside, just her tortured cries. Her eyes hold me. It's as though she and I are the only ones here, like she's brought me back through time and space.

Michael's voice snaps me out of my trance. "Ruby was with the rest of us at the funeral. We all went our separate ways afterwards, planned to meet back here at five."

"It happened within the past half hour," the detective says smugly. "That means right after the funeral. It makes a number of people here suspects."

"I was the first one here—besides Ernest. He was out back mowing the lawn. Oblivious to everything as usual," says Linda through sobs. "I called the police. That damn detective really grilled me, Ruby, don't let him get to you." Shelly has his arms around her. Ernest is staring at us and biting his nails. There's something wet on his right sneaker. I don't see Max or Miles anywhere.

Detective Mansi shakes Michael's hand and peers into the ballroom as he peels off a pair of white plastic gloves.

Two men with macho stances.

The room is sealed off with yellow police tape. A group of uniformed cops are standing around something—or someone—on the floor. I see a camera flash going off.

"What's going on?" I ask.

"Mary was alone in the ballroom. Somebody cut her throat," the detective says bluntly.

"Wha—"

"She'd been painting for the past few days. Seascapes, of all things. Best work she'd done since she'd been here. The killer poured some of her blood, hair and nails into a cauldron and left it beside her. The detective says it's the same MO as the other murders. A detail they leave out of the news," Shelly chimes in.

"Cody Bartman," says Linda wiping tears from her eyes.

"Who?" I say.

Detective Mansi is now standing a few feet away from us. He's listening intently.

Linda speaks softly. "From my research books about the area. In the early sixties, there was a series of murders at the University of Rhode Island. Man name of Cody Bartman— who supposedly practiced black magic—used to stab the girls—right in their dorms, then he'd drain some of their blood, clip some nails and hair. Leave it all in a cauldron by the dead girls' bodies. He told the police when they caught him that each girl had hair like the woman he loved. Each one was a psychology major. Seems he was in love with his shrink. He said by killing them he'd eventually win her love. Claimed the blood, hair and nails were offerings."

"I remember reading about that years ago," says Michael.

"We've already found the similarities," says the detective. "Some copycat nut. We'll get him—or her." He looks first at Linda, then at me.

Anger burns in Linda's eyes. "You've got to be careful with this stuff, detective. One book I have says the spell worked. The shrink visited Bartman in jail, even cried the day they gassed him. She hung herself six months later and left a note saying she was joining him."

Mansi shakes his head. "Nonsense. The shrink got married and is still alive."

"Believe what you want." Linda glares at him.

"Enough with this jive."

I hear the screen door slam. The lady in green looks startled. She quickly vanishes.

"Gallo, good to see you," says the detective.

"Glad you came, Joey," Michael says.

"Cops outside told me what happened. How much more death can we take?" He reaches for Linda's hand.

"We'll be fine, Joey," Michael says. "We just need to stick together."

Joey turns to Detective Mansi. "You've got to find Gracie." He backs into the wall, slides down, puts his hands over his eyes and weeps.

Detective Mansi shakes his head. "Joey, we're doing all we can, sport."

Ernest backs away. He almost seems to slither up the stairs. Nobody notices but me.

I leave Michael and the others talking. I stand at the bottom of the stairs, watching Ernest enter one of the bedrooms. I walk up the stairs quietly.

I peer into the room. Ernest's little dwelling. I can tell by the New England Patriots poster hanging on the wall. He slides his hand into his pocket then takes a deep breath as he removes something shiny. He lovingly strokes a treasure, kisses it tenderly.

Mary's bone necklace.

I quietly turn. Then I tell Michael and the detective what I saw.

There's blood on the necklace. The police handcuff Ernest and lead him to one of the cruisers.

"I loved Mary," he says through tears. "I took the necklace because I wanted something of hers."

After a few hours of questioning, Detective Mansi informs Michael that it's best that Ernest stay in state custody—they have facilities for people like him— until he's either cleared—or until they find more evidence pointing to him.

I'll meet Michael back at my house for dinner. I just want to walk on the beach now, and reflect. I feel my knife pressing against my leg. How quickly could I grab that knife if something went down?

It's all a mystery—every damn bit of it.

One thing stands out in my mind, something I can't quite put my finger on. It happened before I left Green Briar today. As I made my way to my van Detective Mansi came up behind me. He took my elbow.

"Before you leave, Ruby, can I ask you something?"

"What? If I put a black magic curse on this town when I came here—if I've brought the Devil to Nazareth?"

He looked at me as if he may have been wondering just that, but said, "There's something else—"

An image of Mrs. Hudson flashes through my head. "What?"

I heard a door slam. Michael stood on the porch, arms folded and looking our way.

Mansi acknowledged Michael with a slight wave. For a moment disappointment flashed in his eyes. "It can wait."

"Detective, I had nothing to do with any killings. I'm not an angel, but I'm not a killer."

"Never said you were." He smiled at me and walked away.

I looked at Michael and shrugged my shoulders. He looked annoyed.

Things are going to hell.

What happened to all the magic?

17

THE TELLING CIRCLE

We've been opening up to each other more since the deaths. We've continued our *Tellings*. It's our way to heal. It's helping. It really is.

Michael has spoken about his mother. She died of breast cancer two years ago. He visits his father in a nursing home in Warwick as much as he can.

I haven't said anything about Johnny. Never will. Charlie Hurd, he was special too. He was my dad's younger brother and my godfather.

Uncle Charlie used to bring me dolls—gifts from trips he took to Europe—French, German and Italian, all collectibles I cherish and still have. I've always wondered if he really bought them or if he lifted them.

Charlie and my dad used to drink whiskey and talk about elaborate scams they'd pulled off when they were younger. They'd set up fake jewelry appraisal companies in different cities, do extensive advertising about cut rate prices. Had fake credentials. Some people fell for it and left their valuables in the hands of two of the best scam artists I'd ever met. In the end, my dad and Charlie would possess a fortune in priceless jewelry and they were long gone before the heat was on.

Charlie died in a car crash, while being chased by a state trooper on the Jersey turnpike. I told the group about my uncle, the dolls and how much I loved him, leaving out the part about the chase—and his *partnership* with my dad.

The red candle's flame has turned a brighter orange and

flickers gently back and forth.

Max smiles at me. "I get the feeling that you miss your dad a lot, don't ya, Ruby?"

"Yeah, lots."

Max has a strange look on his face, like he's going to break down and cry. "I had family, a sister. Her name was China. She had red hair like mine. Pretty kid, but not right. My mother was a prostitute in Boston where we were born. Strung out on heroin the whole time she was carrying my sister.

"My mother left us when I turned eighteen. China was fifteen. Guess Mom figured I was old enough to take care of things. China was so innocent." He cracks a smile. "The state paid for her medication and doctor visits. They sent us a monthly check for housing and food. I did odd jobs for extra cash. That's how I met Max."

I see a vision of Max and Miles breaking into a house, opening drawers, dumping out the contents, then stuffing cash into their pockets.

"China and I used to take a cab from our flat in Dorchester to the children's hospital in Boston. She'd climb in the front seat and introduce herself to the driver, then she'd turn to me in the back seat and say, 'This is my big brother, Max.' They'd always laugh. One afternoon she was sitting on our front steps. I imagine somebody stopped and opened the car door. She got in like she was going to Boston." His voice cracks. "They found her body two weeks later stuffed in the trunk of an abandoned car by the train tracks near Boston Garden. She'd been raped and tortured.

"After that Miles and I headed south. We got into trouble while passing through Providence. Got thrown in jail for some of our *antics*. We ran into Michael and he convinced us to come to Green Briar. We didn't get too far in our travels, but that's fine with me."

"Fine with me too," says Miles. "My own Ma was like Max's. Lived on money she made from selling her body. Never knew my Dad. She told me he was a dealer from Cape Cod. I never had much loving from her. She was always tense, nervous about paying the bills, about her pimp being on her case. I was her son and she fed me, made sure my bed sheets were clean. Occasionally she'd bring me a box of good chocolate or a half gallon of expensive ice cream." He gulps, closes his eyes for a second. "I loved her though. She was the only thing in the world I had. She was a white woman named Mollie who gave birth at fourteen.

"When I was sixteen she told me she was gonna get away from hooking. The state would help her. They had some programs. I remember her face, how her eyes glowed when she told me she was going to learn to read, get her high school equivalency. Get a real job. 'I'll be a real mother to you, Miles,' she told me.

"Her pimp got wind of her plan. Beat her death. Last time I saw Mollie she had that glow in her eyes. That's how I want to remember her."

Funny how we all deal with death differently. We all have our ways of remembering, of feeding our love to the candle's flame.

18

LINDA'S CONFESSION

I'll be having dinner with Linda tonight. We're going out for a pizza. later we're going to browse around the herbal shop on Route 2. Michael's out with Shelly, said he'd be by later on.

"Why haven't you spoken in our circle yet?" I ask. She's drinking tea and thumbing through one of her books; *Serial Killers of Canada.*

"My grandmother died when I was thirteen. She died of old age. No dark, gritty details. She didn't even suffer like Michael's mother. Just passed away in her sleep. I don't remember my other grandparents. There's nobody else, except a pet parakeet."

"Just talk about your grandmother, you loved her, didn't you?"

"Yeah, but I feel that the others have more pain. I was a pampered kid from an upper middle class family. The others need more healing. My life has been boring, except for my writing, my books and my imagination."

"Why do you stay at Green Briar? You're different. I sensed that the first time I met you, despite your clothes and your literary tastes."

"Research, I guess. I left St. Louis, Missouri two years ago. My intentions were to travel on the road with my boyfriend. He played guitar for a band. I was going to write a novel about life on the road with a musician, add some details about how a lot of people get hacked to death along the way."

"Charlie Starkweather kind of stuff?"

"Yeah, it was going to be a bestseller. Only thing is this guy,

Ed, dumped me at a concert in Providence."

"How'd you end up at the house?"

"I went to an all-night diner, was getting high on caffeine. Crying my eyes out. Nobody noticed me at three in the morning. Everyone there was either drunk or half asleep. But Shelly walked in and spotted me.

"He bought himself a cup of coffee then sat down with me. Told me he didn't mean any harm, but if I needed somebody to talk to, he'd listen.

"He listened to me until five and I listened to his stories about Green Briar and the people there until seven. He said if I didn't have money, or anyplace to go, then Green Briar would welcome me. Truth is I did have money and family who'd welcome me back, but the house sounded like a James Leo Herlihy novel. Remember *Season of the Witch?*"

"Yeah."

"I felt if I spent some time there, then maybe I could write something worthwhile, not some cookie-cutter slasher book. So, I accepted his offer."

I laugh. "You're a scam artist and you don't even know it."

Linda laughs. "Guess so. Maybe we've all got smatterings of the Devil."

"Yeah, we sure as hell do."

Why is she looking at me with that knowing smile? I'm sure she wants me to confess some of my deep, dark secrets. I refuse.

I grab my sweater. "Come on, girl, let's go buy some herbs."

"Can we stop at the bookstore too?"

"Sure."

"I heard that Hollywood is releasing a new movie about *Jack the Ripper*. The detective on the case was Frederick Abberline. In the script, he solves the crime through dreams. Of course, the killer is a rich man and it never goes public." She opens her purse and counts dollar bills. "There's a book on it I want to buy."

"A psychic detective. Just like Mansi."

"Mansi is the most unimaginative man I've ever met. He's rather an ass, too."

"You got that right."

Solving crimes through dreams? Maybe I'm not crazy after all.

"Something else I remember about it—there was evidence that Jack was a ritual killer, same as Bartman. Same as a few other serial killers. Strange, isn't it?"

I think of the cauldron they found by Mary. I wonder what kind of dreams I'll have tonight.

19

MORE BLOOD

August 31st

I had an odd dream last night. I was in the ballroom at Green Briar. Johnny was there too, looking as though he'd just risen from the grave. His face was white and there were black circles around his eyes. His hair was greasy and slicked back. He wore a black suit, covered with dirt and dried pieces of grass.

That damn song was playing, *Putting On The Ritz,* and Johnny was dancing round and round by himself. One by one Mary, Dean and Shelly's Maya filed into the ballroom. They joined Johnny. All of them were dressed in black. Grass and sticks were in their hair and they had blackened eyes.

Johnny spun around like a whirling top. The others watched him, swaying back and forth. Their faces had no expression. When Johnny stopped, he wasn't Johnny anymore. He was the Cody Bartman from the poster I saw in Pearl Bones, complete with bloody knife and flaming cauldron sputtering in the background.

He took Mary into his arms, carried her to the pot and threw her in. She disappeared into smoke and fire. Then he started walking towards me, the music cranking up louder and louder, faster and faster like somebody turned the speed up on an old record player.

I woke up before the song ended and damn if I can get it out of my head now. What the hell did it mean?

I sip my morning coffee and remember the way they all

moved around the floor, like zombies. I look at my calendar and see today's date circled in red. Matty jumps on the table and meows. I hear Lady Lucy humming outside my window.

Where's my bag of tricks? It's time to do my spell.

A strand of Michael's hair. A strand of mine. I shake the bottle filled with holy water, a souvenir from *St. Rose's* down the road. Apple seeds. A plastic Saint Barbara. Am I supposed to say a rosary after I'm done with all this? I hope I can remember how.

I sprinkle the holy water, ask Heaven and Earth to make things right. Not only for Michael and me, for the dead, for Gracie and for everyone in our circle of friends. Now where can I bury all this stuff?

Matty sniffs and then stretches out on a grassless spot. He looks up at me as if to say, *This is the place.*

I kneel beside him. The dirt is soft and loose here. Good a place as any.

Somebody must have been digging here recently. This is much too easy. The dirt is moist and easy to manipulate. Lady Lucy said to find soft earth, didn't she?

There's something here.

Gracie's silver necklace with the cross that her father gave her. The blouse she was wearing the last time I saw her—what looks like blood stains on it. Her book of poetry. I touch the blood on her blouse, my fingers tingle, there's a pounding in my head, like an intense energy rushing through me.

Some things will be uncovered, but there's more beneath the surface.

Michael pulls up in his truck. He has takeout from *The Fish Market* around the corner. I can smell fresh haddock and chowder.

Matty sniffs the air. Sniffs the contents in the grave. Growls at Michael.

I stand there frozen. Prayer beads, apple seeds and a plastic saint at my feet.

Lady Lucy wanted me to find these things. That day, when she came to the shop, she said something to me about things being uncovered and dreams being set in motion.

"Ruby—what's wrong? What the hell are you doing?"

"It's Gracie stuff. I think there's blood on it." Michael's face turns white. Tears well in his eyes. "This doesn't mean anything. She could have just buried her things here. She's a clumsy kid. Could be cherry soda—her favorite—spilled all over everything."

"She never took that cross off, Michael—she said she never would."

"I'll call the station—talk to Mansi. Let's just leave everything as is, never know if we're damaging prints or DNA, or whatever they look for."

"Okay," I say as I gather the ingredients for my spell.

Thunder rumbles. Rain suddenly begins to fall. Joey's car pulls up behind Michael's truck. "Oh, great, if he sees this stuff he'll freak."

"Let's just walk over there, let's not let him near here."

I notice his face is thinner. He looks unkempt. "He looks kind of out of it anyway. I think we can pull it off."

Matty stays close by me as we walk towards Joey. He growls softly.

"Michael, Ruby. Sorry to just barge in, but can I join you guys for supper? I'm feeling real low. I could use the company."

"Joey, sure, we'd love the company," says Michael.

"Yeah, I even baked a pie," I say.

"Let's get inside. We'll light some candles—pray for the best," says Michael. I wish I had his faith. I envy his strength. I can't tell if those are tears or raindrops trickling down his face.

Michael—he's such a decent man. I often think he's too good for me. He doesn't know about my past. I wonder if he'd even care.

On the other hand, it feels as though Detective Mansi had me figured out the minute he laid eyes on me.

Damn Mansi. What does he want from me anyway?

20

DREAMS OF A KILLER

Tonight, I dream of Cody Bartman again.

He's standing in the middle of the ballroom at Green Briar. Michael's silver knife is in his hand. There are dead chickens on the floor. Mary sits cross-legged and is praying on Mrs. Baldwin's rosary beads. Cody Bartman is walking towards me.

Got to make her mine forever. That's why I kill, to make the love stronger. Now it's your turn to die.

I try to run, but can't. I can hear Gracie's voice beneath me. I hear pounding on the floor, like she's banging on a ceiling below my feet. Bartman lunges for me. A hand jerks me away as the point of the blade touches my throat. The lady in green hands me a card. It's blank. A drop of blood drips from its edge.

Now Johnny and I are walking. I see a sign. It tells me we're in Point Judith. We can catch the ferry boat to Block Island from there.

Ferry's not running tonight, says Johnny.

He points to a street sign.

Sword. There's something else there, but his index finger is covering it.

"Is that a real street? Or a symbol for something?" I asked in my dream voice.

Could be both says Johnny as he levitates above a church steeple.

"Come back—where—" I'm holding Gracie's bloody blouse. It's wet and my fingers are smeared with red. I feel tingling, pounding and an electricity running through me. The street sign glows in the dark. The Seven of Swords from the tarot deck dangles on a thread from the pole. I hear a weatherman talking about hurricane season, storms brewing on Narragansett Bay, beach houses being boarded up, and people having emergency supplies in their basements.

Johnny kisses me. Gotta fly away. You'll know soon— then you need to go.

This morning I take my time, getting dressed slowly and then holding Matty in my arms, finding comfort from his gentle purring.

I've given Mrs. Baldwin a key to the shop. She'll open for me—has been for a while now. Linda has been helping out as well as Max and Miles. I pay them what I can out of the profits. Mrs. Baldwin gets these *hunches.* Not schizoid dreams, or visions like mine. She just *knows* things. The others all know some form of divination—tossing cowrie shells, Runes, Miles can even read astrological charts a bit. He's been studying with Shelly. He can do a basic reading. All he needs is an exact birth time.

I've taught them all the symbols of the *Rider Waite Tarot.* Low and behold not one of them is a shabby Tarot reader. Surprisingly enough nothing is ever missing from the register or from the stock.

Joey Gallo has been frequenting the shop. He's become addicted to my readings. He keeps asking if I see Gracie, if I think she's okay. He won't let anyone else read for him. He's a tough one. I don't get many vibes from him. Happens with some people—you just can't read them, but I humor him anyway, telling him that he'll find true love—telling him everything is cool. Somehow, I don't think there's good things in store—not for Joey anyway.

20

TEA WITH DETECTIVE MANSI

Today I arrive at the shop about ten. Candles and incense are burning—just the way Dean did it. Miles is reading a book on Moon signs. Linda is setting pewter angels on a shelf next to some new candles. Mrs. Baldwin is on the phone—sounds like she's making a bet. Max is waiting on a customer—an old woman who's purchasing a crystal unicorn.

Everything looks normal, but nothing ever is of late. Michael comes by about three—after school lets out.

"The blood on Gracie's blouse belonged to Dean. Mansi got the report about an hour ago. He called me on my cell phone as soon as he knew. He's put out an all-points bulletin for her. He says she's a very credible suspect."

"I still don't think she did anything."

"Me either. Mansi been around here asking questions?"

"No, not yet."

"Okay," he says, then gives me a peck on the cheek. "I'll cook you dinner later."

Around five Mansi arrives. The others have all left. I'm having a cup of tea, just getting ready to call it a day and meet Michael back at the cottage.

"Good day, Ruby."

"Want a cup of tea?" I should probably be polite to him.

"No thanks, but I'll sit with you—if you don't mind."

"No harm."

He sits too close. He smells of good cologne.

"What can I do for you, Detective Mansi?"

"You can call me Andrew."

"What's up, Detective Mansi?"

"Gracie. She confided in you. She tell you anything about having a knife? She practiced that heebie jeebie crap too, didn't she?"

"It's Santeria and, no, I don't think Gracie had a knife."

But I *do* have a knife. What would he think if he knew that?

He taps his fingers on the table.

"Kids. So defiant at times. I was in a bit of trouble when I was Gracie's age. I turned myself around. Now I'm a law officer. I never thought I'd be doing this kind of thing when I was younger."

"People change, I guess."

"Exactly. Nobody's good or bad. It's just circumstances, just the way life works. You and me—we could mesh. We're more alike than you'd like to admit."

I don't answer. Anger is burning inside. He's got balls. He stands. "Good day, Ruby."

"Bye, Detective Mansi."

The chimes jingle. The door closes behind him.

"Asshole," I say to a ceramic dragon on the shelf beside me. "Mansi, you're such a prick."

21

9/11

I can smell the ocean through the open window. This will be a lovely and mild September according to the weatherman. I swear I can feel tiny flutters in my stomach now, but the doctor says it's early for that yet.

The tourists have left Nazareth. Pearl Bones still does well—especially on weekends. The horrid happenings here made more city people curious about the town and the shop.

I feel another flutter.

I'm going to tell Michael today. He called in sick, said he just wants to hang out with me. I've made my decision—or have I? I wish things weren't so damn complicated.

It's about quarter to nine in the morning. I didn't sleep that well last night. Had this dream that I sat up in bed, looked at my bedroom mirror and saw this intricate web strung across it. Two spiders were in the upper right-hand corner of the web. There was another spider a little further to the left—a tad below the others. A voice whispered, *They worked all night to make this web...*

Now I hear Michael moving around the kitchen.

The radio is still playing. The lull of a reporter's voice suddenly seems to grow louder.

I hear Michael say, "Holy shit."

"Wha..." I say sleepily, burrowing closer to the sleeping cat beside me.

Michael is now in the doorway.

"Plane just crashed into the World Trade Center."

"My God."

"It's the North Tower. Ninety-Two people were on board."

"Did they say if it was an accident. Or….?"

Two spiders were in the upper right-hand corner of the web… The Tower…

"They don't know." He bites his lip. "A tragedy. Fucking shame."

"I'll make coffee."

The clock ticks slowly. I see Lady Lucy strolling down the street. Matty retreats beneath the bed.

The clock says 9:03 a.m..

The radio announcer talks about the rescue workers in New York. About the smoke. His voice cracks as he says, "Another plane just hit the South Tower. Another Boeing 767. There's flames and debris everywhere. This is sheer horror. America has been attacked."

The Tower.

"My New York. Michael—New York."

Michael's face is white. I've never seen fear on his face before. "Come sit down, babe. Let's get it on TV." He takes my hand and leads me into the living room. Gently sits me down on the sofa. Clicks the remote.

There is a war zone in my city.

A rapid succession of horrific events are coming. I can feel it.

My country.

It's 9:43 a.m.

The Pentagon is hit. "Like a bomb blast," they said.

9:58 a.m.

The South Tower collapses.

People are running. The cloud of debris covers everything.

10:28 a.m.

The North Tower is gone. My city.

Civilians, firefighters and policemen are dead or missing. My heart literally aches. A terrorist network is blamed.

Tonight, Michael and I just hold each other. I'm afraid. Afraid for my country. Afraid for the freedom that I've always loved. Afraid for this child growing inside me.

I'm so afraid for Nazareth. I dream again tonight.

Johnny takes me back to the dark basement. This time it's Gracie sitting cross-legged on the floor. She's holding a yellow daisy, pulling the petals off. *He loves me, he loves me not.*

A man, dressed in an old-fashioned police uniform is standing in front of me. He's holding a human heart in his hand. The name *Abberline* is etched on a copper badge he wears on his chest. He writes on a small notepad as he speaks. *They're all ritual murders. My dreams told me. They keep the best stuff in the basements.*

Now Johnny is standing here. *The man who holds The Seven of Swords—Ruby, you know—you know.*

22

THE KING OF PENTACLES

The King of Pentacles surrounded by Swords. Must mean that sooner or later I have to tell Michael about the baby—could mean that he won't be happy once he finds out.

I'm being a fool.

The King of Pentacles is a man with dark hair. The Sword cards imply danger—or heartache.

Seems I can't win here.

I *am* a fool. Since when did I really start believing in the cards?

I've been working at the shop for eight to ten hours a day. At night, I turn on the TV. The news has become so important. I'm afraid that something will happen and I'll miss it. That maybe the whole world will be on the verge of exploding—and I won't know until the last minute.

If it wasn't for Michael I don't think I would have eaten over the past few days. He brings me dinner each night, makes sure Matty is fed and then he sits beside me as Tom Brokaw shows us clips of the New York City skyline—as CNN shows the planes crashing into the towers—over and over again.

I've been getting some pains in my belly. Dr. Benstein, a man in his early forties, with horn-rimmed glasses, and a birthmark on his nose, says it's probably nothing, just the baby stretching my uterus out. He's running some tests on me next week, told me to call him before that if the pains get any worse.

Each night without fail I dream of Johnny. He takes me to the house with the damp basement. The drawings on the walls are so many now that they are stacked on the floor and they hang one on top of the other.

The man who holds The Seven of Swords.

He loves me. He loves me not. Hair, nails and blood.

Gracie's lips form the words and her pen moves swiftly over vellum paper.

Johnny sails away on a Ferry boat, or floats above a cathedral.

Dreams.

Did someone tell me to listen to their meanings?

It's Saturday. Flights in the country are still not back to normal. They've been grounded for days and this morning a scant few are leaving the airport in Warwick. Tuesday's happenings still lay heavy on my heart and mind.

Business at Pearl Bones has been steady. People are buying all kinds of spiritual items—the unique crosses Dean stocked, prayer books from every religion and vigil candles.

Max and Linda are watching the shop today so I can get to the pet store and rent a few videos to take my attention from the news. The mood is somber everywhere. People are more patient. When a clerk at the grocery store jams the register, and holds the line up for ten minutes I tell the woman in front of me, "Things like this don't bother me now."

"No," she says. "It's okay to wait. It's really okay."

In the pet store the woman tells me that they've already raised three thousand dollars for the Red Cross. I try to say something to her, but I only end up holding back tears.

I now have cat food, videos and a new pair of gloves. The colder weather is approaching and my hands always get so dry. I turn the corner to make my way onto the highway. There's a dead cat lying in the road.

I cry all the way home.

23

LISTEN TO MY DREAMS

The weeks unfold as the events of September 11th and the murders overshadow our lives. Gracie is still missing. Ernest cut his wrists last week. He got hold of a carving knife from the kitchen at the state home. It was too late when they found him. It's always too late.

Michael still doesn't know I'm pregnant. I'm just afraid that he'll have a hold on me once he finds out, but I don't know how much longer I can hide it from him. He's been telling me I'm getting fat. I tell him it's all the good food I've been eating.

The tests my doctor ran didn't show anything negative.

"Just take it easy, Ruby. Eliminate stress as much as you can. Walk twenty minutes a day. That'll all help."

It's not helping. I still feel like hell.

Mansi comes by Pearl Bones often.

He's here now, speaking in hushed tones to Joey, who's been here since we opened, just rocking back and forth in Dean's old chair in the corner. Joey looks up at the detective with red-rimmed eyes. His voice is soft. His face lacks any kind of color these days.

The detective pretends he's looking at the candles and the books. I know he's looking at me. I know he thinks I have something to do with it all.

He saunters over. "You into witchcraft, Ruby?"

"No, I just read cards and I've inherited Dean's shop, so I like to stock the same kind of merchandise he did. None of it relates to witchcraft. It's all harmless."

"Sure it is," he says, turning to Linda.

"This Santeria stuff, wasn't there a movie about that a few years ago? Weren't they going to sacrifice a kid?"

"*The Believers*, says Linda. "Hollywood hype. The real practitioners of Santeria haven't an evil bone in their bodies. There's some books here if you want to read up."

"I like reading about American history, once in a while a good mystery, not that fantasy, devil worship stuff."

"Creep," says Linda when the detective is out the door.

"I think he hates women," I laugh out loud—the first time since September 11th. "Maybe *he's* the killer."

"Yeah, could be," says Linda. She reopens the book she'd been reading—*Jack the Ripper, Letters From Hell.* "Detective Abberline should be on this case."

I follow Mansi out the door. I need to get something off my mind.

He's lighting a cigarette and looking up and down the street at the artists selling their wares.

"Vagrants," he says. "But they have first amendment rights, so we can't arrest the sons-of-bitches."

"No, you can't," I say defiantly, then I smile my smile. "Look, Detective, I know you think all this mystical stuff is bunk, but I've been having dreams—"

"Well, Ruby, you're right, it is bunk. I don't think your dreams will tell me anything, nothing at all. What do you want, money or something? Are you trying to scam the police department with this nonsense? I thought you were smarter than that."

"No, I'm not scamming anyone. Look, just check this out. Is there a Sword Road—or Sword Street someplace down by the ocean—in Point Judith? If there is, then check out number seven. Check out the basement."

"And what will I find there? Another body? A witch's coven? What?"

"You check out hunches, don't you?"

He laughs in my face then shakes his head, pulls up his jacket collar and makes his way to his car.

Michael is sound asleep by my side. Matty is lying on the floor at the foot of the bed. I can hear Lady Lucy singing outside, her jewelry jingling. Every now and then thunder rumbles in the distance.

Ruby, it's almost over.

Almost time to hit the road.

Johnny.

Here he is, just standing here, looking down at me with ghost eyes.

Close your eyes and I'll show you things.

I close my eyes and Johnny touches my hand. We walk. Before long another joins us—Death, hooded, carrying a scythe in one hand, a book in the other. He opens it and begins to read. He tells me who'll be the next to die, then he kisses me and flies away with Johnny. It's like a Marc Chagall painting—green and red with fantasy wings. Blue horses and fiery cathedrals emerge from the clouds and the moon smiles as they pass by. On and on they go, leaving me standing here on Earth. They soar. Over Nazareth. Over New York. Over the milky way and then to Hell.

24

SORROW

October 9th

I don't feel good at all today. I had a few sharp pains this morning, put in a call to Dr. Benstein's answering service. It's Sunday, don't even know if he's around.

He gets back to me in twenty minutes.

I tell him I had some pain earlier, now I just feel drained.

"Take it easy today. I want you in my office at eight in the morning. If the pain continues check into Saint Joseph's hospital I'll be there as quick as I can."

Maybe I'll feel better if I get out for a while.

I need underwear. My belly is hanging over my bikini briefs. My breasts are swollen and I think I'm at least a cup size larger. Gross, but a fact of life I guess. I haven't bought anything new in a year or so. I drive to the mall up in North Kingstown. White and lacy things—that's what I want. The clerk, a flat-chested redhead shakes her head as she measures my breasts.

"Small bosom and waist. Large cups. You got it going on, girl."

Yeah. I wish I had it going on.

On the way home, I stop at the shop. Linda is waiting on a customer.

"Hey, Ruby," she says. "News said earlier that something big might be going down later. Turn it on when you get home."

"The news is always on lately, girl—you know that."

"Joey was looking for you. Said he needed a reading bad.

Said he was out all night—just walking."

"Joey needs a shrink, not a card reader."

"Mansi was in too."

"What kind of questions did he ask today?"

"He wanted to know if you'd be in. I told him you were with your man. I swear he's got the hots for you."

"Not my type. Besides I got some things brewing here." I pat my belly.

"You told Michael yet?"

"No, but I think he suspects."

"Don't you love him?"

I don't answer. I just want to get back home.

I take off my boots and fling them in the corner of the bedroom. I turn on the TV. They're bombing Afghanistan. I wonder if Michael has heard. It's about time we let go on the fuckers.

It's time I let go too.

Now I'm staring at an empty canvas. Paint in juicy piles on the palette before me. Scenes of this beach town in my head. The people. The way the clouds drift over the ocean. Other images manifest as I work. I dip my brush into the vibrant colors. I paint. Often literally throwing globs of it on the canvas. I wonder if this is the way Van Gogh felt when he did those textured paintings with layers and layers of color.

Let it go, Ruby.

I think I feel better. No pain all day. Maybe I'll even cancel the appointment with Benstein.

Scenes of missiles flaring in the air. The commentators voice rising above the sound of explosions.

Just let it go.

I've been painting for three hours. My jeans and blouse are splattered with red, orange, blue, and green paint. The image is oddly enough of the crazy old woman, Lady Lucy. She's beneath a night sky, a crescent moon hangs above. There's a street sign in the distance— *Sword*—the rest of the letters are obscured by mist. Johnny's ghost floats above it.

Lady Lucy's mouth seems to be moving. Her fingers flick back and forth. Strange, but she's got *my* eyes. I can't remember what color her eyes are, the shape of them, only that they are set within wrinkled slits.

I hear Michael's truck pull into the driveway. I hope he's brought something to eat. I'm starving.

There's a knock at the door. Strange. He must have forgotten his key.

I notice that Matty is standing on the counter and ready to pounce up on the refrigerator. "Bad kitty, I'll deal with you after I let Michael in."

Another knock.

"Joey."

He looks like shit. His shirt is torn at the collar. His dress pants are splattered with mud.

"I've been walking all night."

I peer out into the driveway. Michael's truck is there, but I don't see him.

"Hey, Michael picked me up. Invited me to eat with you guys. Said he'd be back in a bit. He wanted to walk a while—let off some steam. He had a tough week, so he's going to *The Fish Market* on the corner to get us some dinner."

I shrug my shoulders. It's something Michael does on occasion and this past week *had* been stressful at school.

"So, what's up?"

"I know this isn't kosher. I should have waited until you were at the shop, but I need a reading. Michael said you wouldn't mind."

"Well, I'm in the middle—"

"Ruby, it's now or never. Please."

"Okay, come into the kitchen."

The cat has succeeded. He's perched on the fridge, sniffing the maraca that Michael gave me last summer. I'd forgotten I put it there. I'll move it later.

Joey's eyes are watery and red. He's been crying. His hands are shaking.

"Sure, come in the kitchen. Looks like you could use a cup of coffee. too."

He walks slowly. His eyes are closed. He shakes his head back and forth like he's reciting a prayer in his head.

I shuffle the deck. I feel more emotion coming from Joey since Dean's death, almost like it was welled up inside him and now it's erupting.

First card. The Devil. The Devil's chains clink together. The two women at his side cry tears of blood.

Joey watches my face. "What Ruby? What do you see? Do you see Gracie?"

"Don't know yet." I turn over another card. A cramp spreads across my belly. Not now. Please not now.

The Ten of Swords. A man lying face down on the ground. Ten swords protrude from his back. The man turns his head. He looks up at me. Dean.

"Okay," I say as I shuffle and then give him the deck. "Just pick a card."

"Any one."

"Any one at all."

His hands are shaking. He gingerly removes a card from the middle of the deck. Holds it out in front of him. The Seven of Swords. A man—with Joey's face is sneaking away, looking as though he's stealing the swords he holds in both his hands. Blood pours from the tips. A shocking realization hits me.

I look up at Joey. Tears are spilling down his face.

"You. The swords. It's *you*."

"At first—when Michael picked me up—I thought I'd come here to ask you to call the cops. To get somebody to go to my house, but after I thought about it…. Down in the basement—down in the basement—Gracie—"

"Where's Michael? Oh shit." There's a series of stabbing pains in my stomach. I feel the color drain from my face. I'm bleeding.

"Fuck Michael. He's fucked now anyway. He didn't care about Gracie, but I do. I do and I can't give up on her, Ruby. I've got to make it so our love will never die, use the essence of the blonde artists, their blood, their nails and skin, the spirit of their art." He looks at the paint splatters on my clothes. "Cody Bartman had the right idea about it all, but they didn't give him a chance to finish what he started. His formula seems to be working. The spell is potent. Don't you know that blood sacrifices have the most power?"

"You didn't hurt Gracie. Tell me you didn't."

"She's safe. She's the only one I *can't* hurt. I'm doing this all for her. Didn't I cover my tracks well? You all thought she just disappeared. Nobody suspected anything."

"Joey, you're sick. Let me call somebody. Let's stop this madness."

He gets up quickly and backs into the refrigerator. "I'll make it quick for you, Ruby. You've been good to me." He removes a .44 magnum from his pocket. He looks at the paint on my clothes. "All the pretty blonde artists. I'm giving them all back to the earth. Blood, nails and hair offered to the sky. A balance, my gifts to earth and the great beyond."

"You're fucking crazy. You've perverted beautiful magics to quench sick longings."

"What about you, Ruby? Isn't that what you had in mind? To learn the magic and use it to scam others?"

How'd he know? Dean?

"It's not the same as murder."

"I don't murder. I *sacrifice*. Can't you understand that?" He raises the gun.

My hands were always quick, something my father had always delighted in since I was little. I think I can do this. I reach down for my knife and then remember I took my boots off.

The room lights up and thunder booms. I think I've been shot, but it's just thundering and lightning—it's just another spasm of pain hitting me—then another.

I look to the window. Lady Lucy is peering in, her hands pressed against the glass. Rains drips from a sagging velvet hat. Another flash and a face from years ago stares back at me—a black man—an African warrior.

"Mansi, gotta call Mansi," I cry as my senses numb.

Darkness. Another shot of pain ripples through me.

I'm going to lose the baby if I don't get away from— don't get myself to the hospital.

I remember something Michael told me the night he gave me the maraca.

Just shake it when you're in danger. They say that Shango' will come to help you.

I look up at Matty and see him staring at me with those emerald eyes. His tail flicks back and forth—like he's waiting for my command. I nod my head and he taps the maraca lightly.

Lightning brightens the kitchen like flashing strobes. Three sharp cramps in succession. I don't know if I can hold on much longer.

Thunder rumbles and shakes the cottage.

Joey is talking like a madman. "It's so simple. Bartman had it together. I sacrifice all the pretty blonde artists, gather their essence, then each time I do it Gracie will love me more."

"She loves you anyway, Joey. You didn't need to kill. Oh, God, what have you done—"

I feel like I'm going to faint. Things get blurry, then clear again.

Shango'.

Matty arches his back and then with a lethal kick knocks the maraca off the refrigerator. It hits Joey in the center of the head. His gun flies out of his hand and across the kitchen floor. I gather all the strength I can and I hold out my arms. Matty leaps into them and I run…

It's pouring rain. I pass Michael's truck. The driver's door is slightly ajar. His body is slumped over the steering wheel. There's nothing left to his head. The radio is playing that damn song, *Putting on the Ritz.* There's a book in the driveway. Michael's cell phone lies next to it. The book must have been for me. Must have been a gift. *Paintings of Marc Chagall.*

I hear the cottage door open. Heavy footsteps. Joey.

A shot. Some yelling. More footsteps. I hold Matty tight.

Now Detective Mansi is talking. His arms are around me. Rain drenches everything. Wet fur. Drops on a policeman's eyelashes. His arms are strong. He grips me tighter. Matty's crushed between us, letting out cat cries.

Hands guide me into the back seat of an unmarked car.

Mansi's voice is kind. "It's over, Ruby. Stop shaking, kid. Joey's dead. He can't you hurt anymore. My men just took him down. We got a warrant to search Joey's property. Didn't add up with him from the beginning. Gracie was locked in the basement all this time." He shakes his head. "So much for skepticism. Something I didn't realize—Joey's parent's beach house is at Seven Swordfish Road in Point Judith. Your dreams were right."

I feel a hand touch my own.

"Gracie."

"Ruby—uncle Mich—"

"I know, kid," I say and we hold each other and cry.

"He took me to the house after the ceremony that night, kept me there. He took my dad's cross, my poetry book, my shirt. Dipped them in blood. Said he'd have to bury them, 'cause the earth would drink in the blood. Told me he was doing things to make me love him more. He was crazy, Ruby. Plain crazy."

"He didn't hurt you. He didn't—"

"No. He said it was all for me. Oh, God, Ruby." She reaches for Matty and he snuggles into her lap.

Mansi's voice is soft, more than I ever remember it being. "Got an odd call telling me to check out the cottage after I picked up Gracie. Guy named Mr. Shanga— Shangro—something like that. Thought it was a prank— but, my instincts were talking to me. You know that feeling, Ruby, don't you? I tried to have the call traced— no luck."

"It's *Shango*', Mansi—Mr. *Shango*'—-"

My insides feel as though they've been through a shredder. Blood is gushing freely down my thighs.

Mansi is talking again. His words seem to melt together. He's driving away from here. The cops have put yellow tape around Michael's truck. The coroner's car has arrived. Blue and white lights flash. Windshield wipers cut through the rain.

"Uncle Michael's dead," says Gracie.

Mansi's voice cracks. "I'm so sorry."

The mother of all pains pays me a visit. It feels as though glass is cutting through my stomach.

Blackness overtakes me.

25

A GOODBYE KISS FROM AN ANGEL

I lost the baby and Michael, both on the same day. I'll miss seafood dinners, gentle scolding's about keeping my gas tank filled, and the fluttering inside me. I'll always wonder what would have happened if they'd both lived. Would I have settled? I'll never really know. No matter what, they changed me forever, brought me far from my days in Boston and Mrs. Hudson.

Mrs. Hudson. I never spent all of her money.

Time to head for Atlantic City. Time to leave Nazareth behind.

My things are packed. Gracie is coming along. She's just bringing along a few things to wear. However, her artwork takes up an entire corner of the van. It's okay. I've thrown out lots of the potions and things I once conned folks with. No need for that stuff anymore. I've got a new lease on life now.

I never claimed to be a saint.

I'm just different, that's all. More sophisticated. I did learn a lot about horse racing recently and there's some new deals going down in Jersey.

Linda dropped by to say goodbye. She hugged me, then said something freaky. "You know, Mansi was wrong about Cody Bartman's shrink. She *did* kill herself, leaving a note saying she was joining him. The spell *did* work."

I hug her again. "No, silly, the shrink was just crazy. Stop talking heebie jeebie."

"You sound like Mansi now. Be safe." Linda was crying when she left me.

Anyway, Gracie's at Green Briar now. Just clearing up some loose ends with Shelly. Legally the house is hers now. She tells me she trusts no one more than the old man to be its caretaker.

I know what she means. Shelly is good people.

We'll stop to visit her mother before we leave Rhode Island. Gracie's looking forward to that.

I even said bye to Andrew—Detective Mansi. He's not such a bad guy.

I brush my hair. I haven't cut it since before I got here. Gads, it's gotten long.

I hear the kitchen door creak open. I thought I'd locked it when I came back in. Soft footsteps. I see Lady Lucy behind me in the mirror.

"Goodbye, Lucy," I say. Somehow, I'm not surprised she's come.

Matty flicks his tail and lies down on the floor next to me.

"Good that you're off to find the real Ruby." Lucy cocks her head. "Or are you really Ruby after all?"

I watch her behind me in the mirror. She moves closer. So close now that I can feel her breath on my neck. She puts her hands on my shoulders, then kisses me—so soft, like an angel's breath. Flowers and mint candy. She seems to flicker. Then she fades, like she's been a ghost— a figment of my imagination all this time.

Her voice is far away. "Nobody's perfect, gypsy girl. I see many years of wheeling, dealing and cheating. That's in your blood. Karma will be hell to pay later on, but you're learning to listen to those dreams. In no time at all you'll be master of them. Can't guarantee you'll be able to make the bad things stop, but you'll learn to deal—you'll learn—"

I've had it with bad things. "Just what—?"

I turn around.

"Where'd you go?"

Now there are colored sparks where she stood. Swirling all around me. Settling on me. Making my skin hot where they land and then melting, like they're becoming part of me—settling inside me.

Or are you really Ruby?

26

LANDSLIDE

"Gosh, it's chilly on the boardwalk."

"I wonder what it's like here in winter," Gracie says as she strokes Matty. He snuggles up to her, tucks his paws inside her jacket.

Gambling casinos tower over us. In between them penny arcades, fast food restaurants and nightclubs flicker with neon. "Ahh, here's the place. *Gia's.* Come on kiddo, my connection awaits."

The ocean sprays drops of salt water on us. I smell vinegar on fries and pigeon poop on cement. A beggar crouches by a doughboy stand. I hand him a dollar and he blesses me. Elderly people walk by bickering about whose fault it was for losing so much money on the slots.

"Come on, girl. I'm actually not quite sure what awaits us here."

Gracie hugs Matty tighter. His nose twitches as a teenager walks by. The cat *meows* as the kid bites into a burger.

I open the door, step inside. Gracie stays close by my side. It smells of stale beer and staler perfume in this place. It's clouded with smoke. A woman dances on stage while another woman plays a jazz tune on the piano. The dancing lady sings, *"My name is Francine..."* She's wearing spike heels, and a boa is draped around her neck. The other woman is wearing jeans and a black lace halter.

"Francine, the rehearsals' over. Go back there and get ready for the show. Can I help you?" says a black woman dressed in a red sequined cocktail dress. I know she's really a man in drag.

"I'm looking for Alexa."

"And you are?" A soft sneeze, a dab to the nose with pink Kleenex removed from leather trimmed cleavage. "Allergic to cats."

"I'm Ruby."

"I'm Rose Marie." She extends her hand. There's rings on every finger—a killer diamond on her right index— some quarters in her palm. "Your father said you'd be coming soon. You like Stevie Nicks?"

"Very much," I answer.

Rose Marie wiggles over to a juke box in a corner, plunks down her change.

She gives me the thumbs up, "*Landslide*—it's on here—one of my very favorites."

"*There* you are, kiddo," says a voice from behind the bar—Dad's voice. I don't see anyone though.

"Just rummaging back here. Ahh, I found what I was looking for."

A red-head in a red dress stands up. She has a bottle of Jack Daniels in one hand and a glass in the other.

"Dad. Well, look at you. You changed the hair, the makeup. You look great in that color too."

"Thanks, it's a *real human hair wig*. Got it on Park Avenue in Manhattan. Bought a new blonde one too."

I walk over to him, touch his face. "You need to get rid of that facial hair though."

I laugh. It feels good. "It's really you, Daddy."

"In the flesh, darling. Give your dad a hug." Stevie's voice fills the room.

My father's arms are warm. I feel his love. "Good to be back with you. I've missed you so much."

He takes a swig of his drink. "You're just in time. We've got some good shit going on in the back rooms at night, stuff the gaming board doesn't have an inkling about and it's all gravy, baby."

"Great. Is Vinny expecting me at Hal Darrigan's new casino?"

"Yep. You'll be working the blackjack table with him. The pit boss is on the take, along with a few of the security guys, so it'll be a real easy operation. Your hands still faster than the human eye?"

"Yeah, of course, I'm *your* daughter. In a way, I feel sorry for old Hal."

"Don't get soft on me, girl. Darrigan's an idiot, made too many enemies when he closed down in Vegas and didn't pay his people. Word travels."

Word does travel among thieves.

This stuff is all second nature to me. The life. The deals. The scams and double crosses. The danger.

Dad smiles at Gracie. "And who's this young thing that I'm incredibly jealous of? Look at the body on you, little one."

Gracie laughs. Matty purrs.

"This is Gracie."

"Hello, little girl. I read about most of it in the newspaper. I'm sorry about your uncle. Even sorrier for what that bastard Gallo put you through."

"I like you already," she says.

Dad laughs his hardy laugh. "What about Dean's shop— Pearl Bones— that you inherited."

"Barbara Baldwin is managing it. People from Michael's house—Linda, Max and Miles—have jobs there too. Things worked out okay. All people with special *talents*. I'm sure we'll thrive in more ways than one with the business arrangement."

"Not Barbara Baldwin who is married to Reggie Baldwin of horse racing fame?"

"The one and only. Best on the East Coast. Great setup is it not?"

"That's my girl—always the smart one."

"Yeah, well there's always something or other going on behind the scenes with us, you raised me that way." I squeeze my father's hand. "I was scared that—"

Dad can read my mind sometimes. "No need. It's all been cleared. I pulled it off."

"The cops aren't looking for us?"

"Nope—Mrs. Hudson vindicated us."

"I think this may offer proof. It arrived today."

He pulls a white envelope out of his pocket. The return address is from a Mr. Andrew Mansi.

Dear Ruby:

By now you must have arrived safely in Atlantic City. I want you to know I'm keeping an eye on the shop for you.

By the way, that matter about Mrs. Hudson…

Yes, I knew all along. I put out an APB on you. I knew about the circumstances in Boston.

Seems the missing Renoirs weren't really missing at all. I guess the old broad just did the inventory wrong— misplaced a few things. The paintings showed up in some crates underneath a stack of old newsprint. Both of you are in the clear.

I'm sorry I doubted you, Ruby. I'm a believer now. As of the first of the year I'm transferring back to Manhattan South. The small-town scene just wasn't for me. New York is a short drive from Atlantic City. I may just call on your services sometime… I may just call, if that's okay.

All My Best,
Andrew

An image of Mansi slumped over the wheel of a police car flashes threw my head. The Manhattan skyline looms above him. It's probably best to stay away, can't set myself up for that kind of thing again. I can't make the bad things stop, but I'll learn to deal.

You'll never have a lasting love. Never.

"What's wrong, kiddo?" Dad's hand is cupping my chin.

"You pulled it off, old boy. Good for you."

"Yeah, but I'm getting old. Think my future may be in the club scene later on."

"Bull."

Dad's a great artist. Did I tell you that? He can copy any

master. Just let him alone with the original for a week or so. When we lived in Boston, Dad was true to his own heart. His real self. A lady if there ever was one. Me and Dad a/k/a Mrs. Hudson lived in a brownstone in the Government Center. Old Alexa Hudson was the administrative assistant for security at The Boston Museum of Fine Arts. She had access to everything—keys, masterpieces—the whole shooting shebang. Cops got suspicious when she didn't show up for work one day— that is after they found out some Renoirs were missing for the MFA's storeroom. Detective Mansi or the Boston police don't need to know that Dad just *borrowed* the paintings for a while—and they really don't need to know how me and Mrs. Hudson are related.

Dad pours me a glass of Jack Daniels. Gracie and Matty play hide and seek round and round the bar. Dad's bracelets jingle as he raises his glass.

"I got rid of the gray wig in New York City. But I wouldn't mind playing the feeble-minded secretary again at some point in the future. Those old broads trusted me so much—so did the head honchos at the museum."

"Dad, I love you."

"I love you too, baby." He takes a sip of his drink, then points at Gracie. He lowers his voice. "What about the drug thing?"

"She said she's into her art now. Just did chemicals to be rebellious."

"Reminds me of somebody."

"Me? I nev—"

"Nope—me."

"You still are a rebel."

He pats my hand. "Got a funny feeling about her. Something uneasy there."

"I've been dreaming again. Johnny's been saying things I need to decipher."

"Best to keep our eyes open. So, you'll be staying? Stick with me a while. Settle here and have some fun."

"Just a while."

"Cheers."

27

GOODBYE RUBY TUESDAY

December 16th

I made another birthday. Still here in Atlantic City, still scamming and dealing.

Mansi's been around a few times. He asked me to go to a Broadway play with him. I declined. No way I'm getting involved with a cop.

He told me he's working on this big case, undercover. Some Cuban dealer in Harlem is about to get put away. He just needs a few more weeks.

I got a feeling about that.

Sometimes it feels like the pain is fading, but when an old wound dies, a new one just comes along to take its place. It still hurts when I see old pictures of the New York skyline—where the twin towers proudly stood. When I read the newspaper and it says somebody I cared about is gone forever.

The news. I'm still a junkie. When I'm not at the casino I'm glued to the TV.

I'm not free of the darkness.

The dreams still come. Johnny tells me secrets.

I dreamed of Dean once. He was with a beautiful Spanish woman—his Harlem lover. They were making love beneath an autumn moon, then their flesh began to crack and split. There was nothing left at the end but bones and tufts of dry hair.

I dream of Michael once in a while—most times it's when the moon is full. I dream he's in a place where the drums beat and there's no sorrow. He holds our baby up to the sun and *Shango'* smiles. I force myself to wake up before the Devil shows his face, before he strikes them down and makes things go bad.

Dad's going to give me a little party later. He made my favorite, a chocolate layer cake with piles of cream frosting. The *girls* will all be there, dressed in their finest.

Even Hal Darrigan is coming tonight. Poor sucker. If he only knew how much I steal from his blackjack table, how good I am at cheating and how much his boys help me out. Deep pockets, quick hands, smooth talkers and professional thieves, great combinations. No biggie. Darrigan still makes the bucks. Millions I hear. The boys get a share of whatever I steal and we're all happy.

I make sure Matty has plenty of dry food and water before I head out. I love this apartment. A guy owed my dad money, about two hundred grand, couldn't pay up. Dad sent some people to have a chat with him.

He gave him this apartment building instead. Some of *the girls* are pretty good with their fists. Frank "Francine" Penrose is a great shot. Can shoot off a guy's kneecap from across the street, can blow off somebody's head from a speeding car.

Al "Rose Marie" Cleveland was once a promising hitter on a Boston Red Sox farm team. He could swing that bat and run like a son-of-a-bitch to boot. He got busted for dealing coke to minors. It ended his career, but he can still swing that bat.

Like I said, they paid this guy who owed my dad money a visit. I think his name was Pete, or Pat, or something like that. Anyway, after that visit, he gave my dad this building *all in his best interests.*

Gracie stays in a small room across from me. She's been quiet. She's been talking about Joey, dreaming about being locked up in that cellar back in Rhode Island. She told me she saw Joey once right after she woke up from an afternoon nap.

I'm worried about her. Dad says he still gets funny vibes from her.

It's starting to snow. It was snowing in the dream I had last night. There was blood on the snow and my dad was frosting my birthday cake.

Francine is coming around the corner. She's wearing a white fur coat, leather hip boots and a red scarf.

"How's the birthday girl?"

"Kind of down."

"We'll cheer you up. Your dad has been working on your cake. Gracie's with him, has been all day. We have so many surprises for you tonight." She waves a slender hand. Her nails are painted with red sparkling lacquer. Hard to imagine that hand popping somebody off with a .38. "Oh, by the way, your father is blonde tonight, just for you."

Gia's flashes above us in neon. Francine pushes open the door. A couple of the other girls have come up behind us. There's snow on their shoulders and hair.

"Why are the lights out?" Francine's voice is shrill.

"Weird." I feel a chill go up my spine.

Francine flicks the light switch. A table is set up in the middle of the club. A birthday cake is in the middle. My father is leaning over it, holding his stomach. His blood trickles onto white frosting.

"Dad. God, Dad." I run to him, put my arms around him, and then call out. "Somebody call an ambulance."

Francine calls 911 on the phone behind the bar.

"Oh, fuck." Francine's boots click on the floor. Rose Marie lets out a yelp and follows. The others huddle together at the bar, shock in their eyes.

Dad's face is white. His blonde wig is tilted to one side. Pieces of his *real human hair wig* have been cut off.

The purple dress he's wearing is soaked with blood. "I think I'll live. It's not that deep. But, Gracie."

Sirens scream in the distance. "Gracie. Where's Gracie? Who did this? Oh shit."

He points to a dark corner. I see the outline of Gracie's slim body. Her wrists are bleeding.

Francine is holding her, rocking her. Blood is clotted on her white fur.

Rose Marie shakes her head. "Too much blood gone. Doesn't look good."

Gracie looks to the ceiling, seems to speak to something there. "The spell worked." Her voice is cracking, dying. "I did what you said, Joey."

The juke box lights up, music seeps out. Mick Jagger saying goodbye to *Ruby Tuesday.*

"Jesus, Ruby." Dad slumps forward. Blood gushes out of his wound. I think of Dean and the way in which *he* was stabbed and Gracie—what horrors did Joey put into her head?

The paramedics arrive, put my father on a stretcher. He takes my hand. "Weird. After she stabbed me I could have sworn I saw a guy talking to her. Young, dressed in a suit, slicked back hair. He stood there while she slit her wrists." Dad squeezes his eyes shut. "Is that him over at the juke box?" He touches my lips. "Everything's in your name, Ruby, so you'll know—just in case. Club, apartment building, banks accounts..." He passes out.

They put Gracie's body on a stretcher, cover her with a white sheet.

Snow comes down harder, covers the boardwalk, swirls in the night sky. I'm holding Dad's hand as they wheel him out to the ambulance, his fate unknown.

Like foggy night images, or a modern work of art, nothing is ever really black and white, answers don't always come in time. Mysteries don't always unravel in the dimension where they were created.

Johnny's face shines in the neon lights and I can hear weeping, far away and ghostly. It's the lady in green.

Johnny winks. I've got to accept it, *deal* with it. The ghosts will always be with me—so will the dreams—telling me secrets that can shift and change with a sigh and shuffling bloody cards that foretell everything, and nothing at all. They'll forever haunt me with Death's riddles... with endings that are merely new and darker beginnings.

ABOUT THE AUTHOR

Sandy DeLuca is an American writer and visual artist.

As an author, she is known for dark and surreal prose; often visceral and shocking. She is best known for her work in the horror genre.

She resides in New England at present, living in an old Cape Cod house, sharing that space with five felines. Her house is filled with paintings she's rendered over the years; books, ranging from popular fiction to the dark and esoteric; and an array of oddities she's purchased on journeys to New York City, Boston and Salem, Massachusetts.

She left her day job in the banking industry in 2011, and now spends her days creating fiction and painting.

CROSSROAD
PRESS

www.ingramcontent.com/pod-product-compliance
Lightning Source LLC
Chambersburg PA
CBHW072240190626
46809CB00018B/2859
* 9 7 8 1 9 4 8 9 2 9 0 8 0 *